MARKED BY
HELL

ERIN BEDFORD

Marked By Hell © 2017 Embrace the Fantasy Publishing, LLC

More By Erin Bedford

The Underground Series
Chasing Rabbits
Chasing Cats
Chasing Princes
Chasing Shadows

The Mary Wiles Chronicles
Marked By Hell
Bound By Hell
Deceived By Hell

Vampire CEO
Granting Her Wish

The Celestial War Chronicles
Song of Blood and Fire
Visions of War and Water

Starcrossed Dragons
Riding Lightning
Grinding Frost
Swallowing Fire
Pounding Earth

Her Angels
Heaven's Embrace
Heaven's A Beach

Curse of the Fairy Tales
Rapunzel Untamed
Rapunzel Unveiled

Crimson Fold
Until Midnight
Until Dawn
Until Sunset

MARKED BY
HELL
ERIN BEDFORD

1

MAN, DID I HATE churches. The extravagant stained glass windows, the statues, and the constant need for absolution were more than I could handle. Not to mention, they always depicted me as a wingless man.

That thought made my hand inch to touch my shoulder where one of the scars on my back ended. The sound of screams and laughter permeated my mind causing me to wince. It had been years since I'd lost my wings, but the very thought of it still caused the old scars to ache. I shook my head clear of the images before I fell into the memory completely. Now wasn't the time for self-pity.

"Miss Wiles?"

I jerked my head up, my attention focusing on the priest. From where I sat in the church pew I had to twist around to look at him. Father Patrick was a normal enough looking guy, with dark brown hair and matching eyes. He wasn't remarkable by any account, but in his field of work, I supposed looks weren't everything.

"Please call me, Mary," I quickly removed my booted feet from where I'd rested it on the kneeling ledge in front of me to stand.

"Very well, Mary. Father Dominic will see you now," the priest nodded to me and gestured for me to follow him. I moved out of the pew and trailed along next to the father.

Saint Paul's was one of many Catholic churches in Los Angeles. It also wasn't the first church I'd been to on a case in the last month. Hell, in the last week. For a city named after holy creatures, it sure had its fair share of supernatural crap, which is probably why I had been drawn to it in the first place.

"You know, Mary," Father Patrick started, keeping his voice low and his eyes on alert, "when I had first heard about your service I had to say I was a bit skeptical. Is it usual for a private detective to take on such cases?"

"I assure you, Father, this is right up my alley. It is kind of my area of expertise." I smirked. The good father didn't know just how much it was my area.

My business card said 'Private Investigator for Hire', but what it should say is 'Supernatural Expert'. I handled anything from cheating spouses to exorcisms. Unfortunately, I received more jobs requiring photographing cheating husbands than finding demons. Lately the number of cases coming in for demon exorcisms and hauntings weren't as rare as I would like.

Father Patrick stopped before an office door where a nameplate read 'Father Dominic'. He didn't open the door. Instead he rubbed his hands together in a nervous gesture.

"You must understand our worries, Miss Wiles," his eyes darted around them, his voice as low as possible though still audible, "We're priests. It's in our job description to deal with forces of darkness such as this, but with Father Dominic . . ."

he sighed and ran a hand over his face, "it is a delicate situation that my brothers' and I have found ourselves in . . . being unable to confidently say we can handle this ourselves."

"It's all right, Father," I patted him on the shoulder, knowing the touch would help put him at ease, "Like I said, this is what I do."

The older man nodded and stepped aside leaving me to open the door. Taking a deep breath, I adjusted my leather coat and knocked. When a faint voice said 'Enter', I twisted the handle and prepared for the worst.

Now, most of my cases usually just involved lower-level demons—those who couldn't do more than influence the host— but sometimes there were ones who could take over the host's body completely. Those were a bit trickier.

Father Dominic's possession had been described as a textbook. He had started off fine, going about his duties as normal, and had gradually become moody and unfocused. Then it had warped into distant and secretive.

Many would just say he was going through a crisis and it was a cry for help. But when Father Patrick had called me about one of their parishioners stealing money from the church, I had a feeling it could be related to the Father's possession.

Now, as I stood in front of Father Dominic and felt his dark aura seeping out of him and into the room, I had no doubt that I'd been right.

"Miss Wiles," the father called out to me, his deep timber filling the room. He stood with his back to the door, his shoulders hunched down, the graying hair on his head the only feature standing out. "How can I help you?"

Kicking the door closed behind me, I plopped down on one of the wooden chairs, propping my feet on top of his desk. I rocked back and forth on the back legs and waited. I didn't answer his question because that was what he wanted. Childish? Maybe, but demons were all about getting what they wanted, and the moment you refused to do so was when they showed their true colors.

It wasn't surprising when it took no more than a few moments of silence before Father Dominic's hunched shoulders straightened out and a slight shudder passed through him. The dark aura that had been more of a glow became a void that filled the entire room. If a human had been in the room, the very feel of the aura pressing down on them would cause a violent physical reaction—emptying the contents of their stomach contents onto the floor would be one.

But I wasn't human. Not really, anyway. I might walk, talk, and act like a human, but I wasn't any more human than the demon currently wiggling its way to the top of Father Dominic's consciousness.

"Muriel," the name hissed out of the father's throat, no doubt burning his esophagus in the process. Father Dominic, or what was once him—I had little doubt he was dead now—took slow, agonizing steps around his desk until he stood beside me. I didn't know what his eye color had been before, but the eyes that looked down at me now were filmed over—though, sightless they were not.

I rocked back and forth in my chair once more before setting it down on its four legs. My lips quirked up at the sides as I angled my head toward him. To an observer, it would appear that I was interested in him sexually, but in fact, I was zeroing in on the demon inside who was fighting the father for control over the body.

The souls of many who are possessed are usually cast out almost instantaneously, and even those who hang on only do so for a day or two. Father Dominic must have a strong soul indeed if he'd been able to stay alive this long. Bad news for the demon, but also for me too. It made my job that much more complicated.

"What are you doing hanging around here? Don't you have a sink-hole to furnish?" I crossed my arms over my chest. The interrogation part of the process was always the most fun.

The demon wearing Father Dominic's face watched me for a moment before throwing its head back and laughing. It felt like worms wiggling inside my ears. It shortened my patience and made it a lot less fun.

"I don't see what's so funny about my question. You shouldn't be here."

"Neither should you, Fallen One." It chuckled once more, its eyes roving over me.

Blech. Demons were such lechers.

"I'm not fallen," I snapped, dropping my feet from the desk. My five-foot-nine height barely reached the Father's eyes. "Falling implies you had a choice."

"Choice or not, you are still stuck here like the rest of us. Why don't you leave us be? You could do with some of us on your side." He tried to sound persuasive, but he didn't know he was barking up the wrong angel.

"I wouldn't want you on my side even if it was the only side." As nonchalant as possible, I reached into my pocket and drew out a necklace. On the necklace, wrapped in a piece of an olive branch, was a feather. One of the only remaining feathers from my once beautiful and immaculate wings. A gypsy priestess had made the talisman for me as a way to harness what was left of my holy powers.

On my own, I could remove a demon, sure, but it was a dirty and brutal process

14

that required the use of my holy aura to overpower the demon. The process, while effective, would destroy the host's soul, and I preferred not to do that if I could help it. Thus, the talisman helped to give a nudge gentler than the Jaws of Life.

"We could help you, you know," it continued, not paying any mind to the way I wrapped the chain of the necklace around my hand with the talisman laying in my palm.

"Oh really?" I pretended to sound intrigued to keep the demon talking so he'd be off his guard. It made it so much easier when they didn't know it was coming.

"Yes," its white-filmed eyes leered at me. *That's right buddy give me your full attention.* "We can help you get your revenge. To find—your friend."

My hand paused mid-wrap. Did they really know where he was? It wasn't a secret I was looking for him, so the demon could easily be lying to save himself. Then again, if he wasn't lying, then I would have destroyed a perfectly good chance to get the information I needed.

Still, the demon hadn't said his name. The demon probably only heard I was looking for him and was trying to trick me.

Ramiel, my best friend and commanding officer when I had resided in heaven. I still remember the day I'd heard he had been captured. It was the first time I had felt any emotion other than utter devotion to our cause.

Devastated, I had let the overwhelming feeling get the better of me and had gone against orders to wait for an extraction team. I had raced out of heaven, bound and determined to save him. But I hadn't been strong enough.

The scars on my back pulsated, a constant reminder of my failure to save him, and of my own weakness. I'd vowed it wouldn't happen again. I would never be at the mercy of demons.

"You know, you make a compelling argument," I watched as the demon let Father Dominic's shoulders sag, and I almost smiled before taking a step toward him, "But the problem is. I just don't trust demons."

Before the demon realized what I was doing, I shoved the talisman to his forehead and forced my aura to its focal point. Each piece of me seeped into the father's body, pushing the demon out. It screamed and clawed at me, causing little rips and tears in my aura. It hurt enough that it forced me to back off a bit, and that was all the invitation the demon needed. It beat at me with renewed strength; pushing me back out the way I'd come and with my aura, it spilled out of Father Dominic and into me.

If you've ever experienced claustrophobia, having another being inside you at the same time was like that. Except a million times worse.

If I had been human I would have been in trouble, but since I was only pretending to be human once the demon found its way in, he couldn't find a way out. I doubled over, gripping my stomach where the demon was bouncing about, wild and frantic. Now that he was out of the good father's body, I didn't have to be so nice, but it was still going to hurt like hell.

Steadying myself on the floor, I drew my entire aura into myself, pushing my holy powers to their limits to purge my body of the intruder. It wouldn't kill him because demons without a corporeal body couldn't really ever be killed, which made them a lot like roaches. I could push holy power onto it until judgment day came, but they'd keep coming back. I just had to remember to be ready for them next time.

When the demon finally gave up the fight and was forced out of me and back to the hell fire where it belonged, an overwhelming need to pass out filled me. I glanced up at the petrified Father Dominic, whose eyes were a lovely shade of cerulean blue.

"Well, that sucked," were the only words I could get out before I collapsed on the office floor of a dumbfounded Father Dominic.

2

FATHER PATRICK AND THE other parishioners were so relieved to get Father Dominic back they had no problem calling my assistant, Trisha, to pick me up.

"I still don't know why you don't just get a driver's license," Patricia—Trisha for short—threw her keys down on her desk back at the office. Her blonde hair had been colored black, which she wore in pigtails with hot pink extensions. I was surprised the Fathers' had even let her in the church, let alone allowed her to take me away. Churches could be judgmental like that.

"Why would I do that when I have you?" I trudged along, my strength after the demon samba still MIA. I had to remember not to do that again. The holy powers I did have were far and few between. I didn't need to waste them on low-lives like that demon.

"And you'll always have me, Mare, but what happens if some day—I'm not saying when—I'm not able to get you?" she crossed her arms over her black on black corset top. Trisha was what the humans liked to call quirky. Though, Trisha called it individualism, her clothing ranged from tight corsets and fishnets to plaid school-girl skirts and Mary Janes.

"Then, I'd make do," creaking open the door to my office—which also doubled as my bedroom—I made my way to the bathroom. I'd fixed it up when I'd first rented the place. It had been a one-bedroom with a crappy mold-infested bathroom before I'd gotten my hands on it.

Now, it gleamed with new water fixtures, a full bath and shower, and fuzzy rugs that made my feet sing. There were few things in the human world I cared about. A good bathroom was numero uno.

Turning the water to scalding, I dragged my clothes off my body, each muscle aching from the movement. I hated getting possessed. It always felt like I had been beaten inside and out. It left my insides feeling like they needed a good scrubbing; something even boiling hot water wouldn't clean out.

At least I had a water heater in which I'd dropped a holy cross. Didn't make the water stay warmer longer, but it beat the hell out of doing an aura cleansing every other week. Not that I got possessed that often, but it didn't hurt to be prepared.

Once I'd rinsed off the extra baggage weighing me down, I felt a hundred times better. I grabbed a towel off the rack and proceeded to dry off as I moved through the bathroom and back into my office with a bit more pep in my step.

"Uh, Mare," Trisha sat behind my desk filing her blood-red nails. "Did you forget something again?"

"Hmm?" I bent over and grabbed a bottle of water from the mini-fridge.

"Mary, come on! I'm right here."

I turned my head toward Trisha who was covering her eyes with her hand. I realized what she was talking about. I had forgotten clothes, again.

I'd only been living as a human for the last five years, and while I had acclimated myself to their culture, I still lacked some of the hang-ups that most humans seemed to have. Like modesty and what Trisha called tact.

I didn't understand what the big deal was. We were all animals, and it made no difference to me. Were humans so out of control of their hormones that the mere glimpse of naked flesh would send them into a frenzy? It made me happy I was above all those animalistic urges.

"Sorry," I muttered, grabbing a clean shirt from the supply I kept at the office.

The place I called home only had enough room for a desk and a couch that folded out into a bed. In heaven, I didn't need to sleep at all. The longer I stayed on earth the more sleep I needed. Probably had to do with my powers waning. It wasn't something I really liked to think about. So I slept, ate, and drank like the rest of the planet and got on with what little of a life I had here.

"So anyways, did you get paid?" Trisha pointed her nail-file at me.

Jerking my pants on, I realized I actually hadn't even talked to the father about payment. Money. Another one of the human needs that I didn't quite get.

When I'd escaped from hell, I'd had no idea where I was or how I would get back to heaven. I'd quickly found out that humans weren't as wonderful as the almighty had tried to make them out to be. It took me days to find someone that would help me.

Adara.

The thought of her made me smile. The ex-demon hunter had taken one look at me and knew right away what I was and what had happened. I had no idea how; she wasn't psychic. Either way, it worked out for me. She helped me get a new identity and taught me all about the fancy weapons the humans called guns.

I moved over to my desk and pulled my shoulder holster on. Tucking the Glock 42 into the holster, I frowned at Trisha, "Not exactly."

Trisha frowned. "What do you mean, not exactly? Either you did or you didn't? Please tell me you actually told them they'd have to pay."

"I didn't tell them," I tugged my boots on and sighed, "Can't you just send them an invoice?"

The young girl's mouth dropped open before clamping shut, "Well, yeah. But it won't do any good if you haven't discussed payment beforehand."

"Why?"

"Because," Trisha snapped, "people are in it for themselves. Mare, you know I love your naïve outlook on humanity, but you have to remember there aren't a lot of good people out there. Even priests."

I almost let out a snort. Naïve outlook. Trisha couldn't be further from the truth. It was hard to ignore how much evil was in the world when I could read people's intentions from across the room. Even Trisha had her dark moments, and no one was completely good. There were more bad humans than I thought were worth saving.

"Got it. No more freebies," I nodded, ending the conversation my assistant-slash-receptionist and I seemed to have on a weekly basis.

Seemingly satisfied, the young girl started to click away on my computer, an old Windows 7 that had seen better days. "So, now that that is out of the way. How are we going to make some dough? Rent is due and you are already a month behind."

She moved the mouse around and stared at the pointer on the screen until something caught her eye. "How about a nice and easy background check?"

"A background check?"

"Yeah," Trisha beamed at me, "This rich guy wants you to check out his prospective nanny. Make sure she's not a child-molester or whatever. Easy peasy."

"That sounds more like a Patricia skill than a Mary skill," I came around the desk and leaned over her shoulder to look at the screen.

"Well, yeah, I can do all the online digging, but he wants you to use your 'special gifts'," she air-quoted, "to sniff out if she's the real deal or not."

"What am I? A bloodhound?"

"When it's a four-digit job, you bark and roll over," Trisha smirked at me over her shoulder.

I groaned. I didn't like to use my powers for menial tasks as if I was some kind of circus freak that could jump through hoops on command. I was supposed to be looking for a way back to heaven, not paying bills.

As if hearing my distress, my cell phone rang.

"Wiles," the gruff voice of Sergeant Thompson of the LAPD greeted me, "How's my favorite PI?"

"Hi, Sergeant," I couldn't help but smile at his attempt at flattery, "Just had a holy water cleanse. And you?"

The sound of him choking on what I knew was a cup of coffee permanently attached to his hand, made me grin.

"Really now?" he asked when he finally caught his breath, "Where would you get one of those done?"

"Oh, you can do it at home. I'll have to show you sometime," I winked at Trisha who was having a laughing fit. No one would know it, but the Los Angeles Police Sergeant was a closet paranormal addict. Something that I had easily picked up on and had since used to tease him mercilessly. I found it especially funny since I, myself, was of the paranormal.

"Yeah. You'll have to do that," he cleared his throat and tried to sound all official, "But that's not what I called about. We have a body."

"Don't you usually?"

"Your kind of body."

My kind of body usually meant there was some kind of weird mutilation, or symbols that moved the murder from normal to paranormal—if one could call murder normal.

"Oh. Well in that case. Where do you need me?" Thompson rambled off directions to an overpass near San Fernando. Great. An hour's drive ahead of us and that's if the traffic was good.

"So, do we have a case?" Trisha's eyes lit up with interest.

I snapped my phone closed after thanking the good Sergeant, and grinned, "We have a case."

3

WHEN TRISHA FOUND OUT that we had an hour's drive ahead of us she was just as enthusiastic as I had been, though more vocal.

"If I'm going to be your chauffeur, I at least need some grub."

I couldn't argue with her. My stomach made itself known at the mention of food.

"Fine," I sighed. I even let her pick the place, though I loathed eating anything fried. And I knew she would undoubtedly pick the unhealthiest food possible.

In a peculiar turn of events, I found the longer I stayed on earth sans wings; the more my body reacted like a human. In heaven, eating wasn't just unnecessary but unheard of. The fact that I was becoming more human each day was both terrifying and intriguing. It also lit a fire under me that no hell-hound would ever be able to replicate. If I became fully human would I even be able to get back home?

I wish I knew.

Almost two hours, and a bag of greasy goodness later, we pulled up to the crime scene. Though, calling it a crime scene was being nice. It looked more like a bad snuff film gone wrong.

From the car, I could see more than I liked and was half tempted to cover Trisha's eyes. The policemen and their crew scurried around labeling and photographing everything, many of them only looking from the side of their eyes at the scene before them, as if they couldn't believe it was real.

"Stay in the car," I opened the door and gave Trisha a pointed look. She rolled her eyes as she munched on a French fry.

The overpass looked no different from the next one. Concrete ground and matching concrete pillars all lay underneath the overpass bridge. As I got closer, I realized the only differentiating color from the gray-on-gray was the four-poster bed in the middle of the area.

The dark wood of the posts stood out against the bland background. The sheets—once white—were stained a brownish red. Thick rope made of silken material was attached to each post and to the limbs of the body lying in the middle of the bed.

"Sorry, miss," a wide-eyed cop stopped me with an upheld hand, "This is a closed crime scene. I'll have to ask you to vacate the area."

There was always one person on the scene who didn't know who I was. I usually yanked their chains but with the way the guy's eyes kept darting to the body and back, and since his face was a bit too green for my liking, I held my tongue. Instead, I pulled out my license labeling me as a Private Investigator.

"I'm Mary Wiles, Sergeant Thompson called me in." I shoved the license into the ill-looking cop's hands.

He turned it over and frowned. "Why would he do that?"

Here we go. Every new officer I came across always asked this question. It was as if they were offended that their boss would ask for outside help. Really, I didn't want their jobs. I didn't want *my* job. But try explaining that to a uniform. It didn't help that I was an attractive woman. It just touched all their fragile male egos wrong.

"I specialize in occult cases," I gestured to the scene behind him, my fingers pointing toward the markings spread out around the area in what I could only assume was the victim's blood, "I'd say from just standing here this case screams occult. Wouldn't you agree?"

The officer's eyes followed the direction in which fingers pointed, his face turning a deeper shade of green before he shoved my license back at me, "Fine, but go straight to Sergeant Thompson. I don't want to get fired on my first day for letting a civilian in."

"Thanks," I tucked my license back into my pocket and made my way to where Sergeant Thompson was talking to the coroner. I'd bet my boots that guy would be puking his guts out before I left.

"I don't care if you are on a schedule. We have to wait for our specialist," Thompson argued with the gray-haired coroner, who adjusted his glasses and frowned.

"The body will begin to decompose further if we do not get it back to the morgue in due time. It has been two hours since you called your so-called specialist and they haven't arrived yet. I need to take the body in before it falls apart out in this heat," the coroner waved a hand to fan himself, though I doubted it helped any in the eighty-degree weather.

"We will wait until she gets here and that's final," Thompson crossed his arms over his large linebacker chest and clenched his jaw making the veins in his forehead pulsate.

As the coroner stomped away to wait his turn, Thompson pulled out his phone and jabbed his sausage-sized fingers at the buttons. I waited for him until my cell phone rang in my pocket. At the noise, Thompson spun around.

With his phone still at his ear, he asked, "How long have you been standing there?"

Ignoring the ringing phone at my hip, I shrugged. "Long enough to know why the other departments dislike you."

Hanging up his phone, he shoved it into his phone holster. "They're just impatient. I'm trying to do my job just like them. I can't have them carting off the evidence before the scene has been thoroughly examined, and where were you anyways?"

I sighed, "My office is in South LA, Randall, and I just got off a job. I couldn't get here any faster even if I had wings," It was partly true. Wings were great for short distances but anything more than a few miles and it became a long, tedious workout.

Thinking of wings made my brain hurt. Dried blood, not unlike that on the concrete, filled my mind's eye and was the only thing I could see. The never-ending sound of the metal sawing into the bones on my back rang in my ears. Vurrr vip, vurrr vip.

"You okay there, Wiles?" Thompson's voice cut into the memory and brought me back to the present.

I swallowed down the bile rising in my throat and shook the image from my head. An angel with PTSD was a sad thing indeed. With the blood and carnage not far away, I was surprised this was the first time the memories had flared up.

"Yeah, I'm fine."

"Are you sure?" the first hint of concern made his brows scrunch down, "I don't want you to lose your lunch all over the body."

"No, I'm good," I shook my head and smiled, "wouldn't want the coroner to hate you even more."

"Like that's possible," Thompson muttered before leading me toward the bed.

Now that I was closer, I could tell the body in the middle of the bed belonged to a woman. Or what was left of her. The silken ropes were attached to each wrist and ankle, leaving her spread-eagled on the bed. The fact that she was naked didn't seem to bother anyone. Her body had been torn apart so much that it made discerning what body part was what nearly impossible.

The symbols circling the bed and those painted on the bottom of the overpass were indeed demonic. I wasn't sure what kind of demon. Lower demons didn't care so much for rituals, but the higher ups did.

"I'm assuming someone has checked for penetration?" I asked not looking at Thompson. Men, especially human men, had issues with talking about sex outside of the actual bedroom. Standing at a crime scene didn't make a difference.

"Yes, there are signs of multiple . . . partners," he choked out, his face turning a bit red.

Ignoring his embarrassment, I studied the victim. Only one thought came to my mind while looking at the scene, "She was willing, wasn't she?"

He didn't answer right away, causing me to glance at him. The strange look on his face made me ask, "What?"

"How do you know it was willing? Only our medical examiner is able to decide that," the suspicion in his voice made me pause.

"You call me in because I'm your resident expert in all things occult and supernatural. Now you question me about knowing things that you pay me to know?" I pulled a pair of latex gloves from the community box. Wiggling my fingers into the holes, I waited for Thompson's answer.

Thompson huffed, "I'm not questioning your abilities. This case has got me riled up. I just can't see how a woman would willingly let multiple men do to her what should only be done with someone special. Yet all the evidence points to that she did and was more than eager."

"What makes you say that?" I frowned.

Thompson moved toward the body and pointed a large finger at the remains of her face. What I saw surprised even me.

Though her eyes hung from her sockets and her lips were mutilated, it was obvious by the placement of the stretched skin and muscle that she had been smiling. Not just a, I'm-happy—see-you-smile, but the kind that is usually reserved for intimate moments.

"So," Thompson continued, "we have a female victim who not only let herself be gang banged," he cleared his throat and looked down but didn't apologize for his terminology, "but even while they were ripping her apart, she had a smile on her face. So, either she was drugged off her ass or there's some voodoo shit going on here," he lowered his voice as he said the last few words.

"Well, you could find out the first part once you let the medical examiner take her, but the other part . . ." I trailed off as I caught sight of something on her face. I leaned in closer until I was barely an inch from her forehead. The smell of her corpse decaying in the heat filled my nose, and I fought back the urge to vomit. There, barely noticeable on her forehead, was a marking. One made with a substance I had seen before.

Brimstone. Only one creature would use such a thing in a ritual. Anyone else would be burned by it.

Pulling away from the body, I jerked my gloves off and tossed them in the trashcan they had set up near the scene. I had no doubt in my mind demons had done this to her. As I calculated the moon cycle in my head, I began to suspect this couldn't have been the first victim.

I stopped in front of Thompson and I growled, "How many?"

"How many what?"

"How many other bodies like this one have been found before you called me in?"

I gave a violent gesture toward the woman's mutilated corpse.

Frowning, Thompson adjusted his stance so his hands were on his hips near his gun. "Two. One last month and one the previous month."

"And why am I just now finding out about it?" I almost yelled. Death didn't bother me. Demons didn't bother me. But being purposely left in the dark when I could have done something didn't just bother me, it pissed me off. And no one wanted a pissed angel.

Thompson's face contorted in anger. "You should be lucky I was able to get you in on this at all. You know the higher ups don't believe in all this supernatural hokey. The rest of the office thinks you're a waste of our resources."

I barked out a laugh. It was no secret that Randall Thompson was the only officer on the force who believed that there was more out there than just bad people. The first time he invited me to one of the crime scenes had been a coincidence.

I had been investigating the disappearance of a little girl whose case had run dry when it led me to a similar scene, minus the bed, just as the police had shown up. No one likes a missing kid, least of all a dead one. Thompson had questioned me to within an inch of my life before finally believing me and asking me to stay on retainer.

That'd been three years ago. I'd just started out as a P.I. The fact that I'd gotten a fake identity so easily still astounded me. I would think humans would be harder to fool but the scene before me reminded me that wasn't so.

"Be that as it may, you don't just have some perverted human sacrifice on your hands here. And she won't be the last." I shoved past Thompson and headed back toward my car.

Thompson's footsteps pounded after me. He caught me as I opened the car door, a curious Trisha still sitting behind the wheel. "What do you mean it won't be the last?"

I stepped back from the car, my hand on the door in a defiant move. "This is a ritual but not some ordinary I-want-to-raise-demons ritual. It's a demons-raising-demons ritual."

"And that means?"

"There won't just be one more body, but two. They need five to complete the process. Five souls. *Pure souls.*" I explained. "Does the coroner have an approximate time of death?"

"Five days ago."

I clucked my tongue. How no one saw the woman before now was beyond me, but it aligned with my suspicions. "The full moon. The next one will be on the first night of the full moon."

"How do you know that?" This time it came from Trisha, toward whom I shot a warning glance. She wasn't supposed to know about police business, though as my assistant it was kind of hard to get her to help me if I didn't tell her. Thompson didn't need to know that though.

"Because the moon cycle is good for sacrificing one thing," I pointed back toward the crime scene, "virgins."

4

IT WAS DARK BY the time we got back to the office, which put me in an even pissier mood. It meant my day had been eaten up by driving, and I'd have to catch up on paperwork tomorrow.

Oh, joy.

My office sat on top of a Wiccan supply store. Madame Serena, my landlord, specialized in everything from palm-reading to love potions and aura cleansings.

The first time Madame Serena had seen me, she-had told me I had the purest aura she'd ever seen and had rented me the space without even having to fill out a form. Her business had been booming ever since. Madame Serena called me her good luck charm. I wasn't so sure.

Trisha parked the car in front of Madame Serena's shop so I could get out. The store sign was still lit, telling customers she was still open for business.

"So, you're going to text my mom, right?" Trisha asked me before I could get out of the car.

While my assistant-slash-whatever-else-I-needed-her-be was eighteen, she still had to check in with her parents. Not because they were overbearing or anything, but because she had some interesting past times, like hacking into the mainframe at the pentagon when she was thirteen.

She told me she'd just wanted to see if she could do it. Luckily, the government didn't see her as a threat and even asked her to come on to their payroll to fight against others who might actually mean harm. Since she had just hit puberty her parents had thought it would be best if she finished high school before starting a life she couldn't get out of. Trisha was supposed to get a boring job so it would keep her out of trouble. Little did her parents know . . .

"Yeah, don't worry. I'll make sure they know you were with me and not out planning world domination," I smirked.

"Damn," she snapped her fingers and smiled, "You found me out. But seriously, last time I came home after ten I had an hour lecture about falling into the wrong crowd. Like, hello? I don't need to leave my desk for that."

Laughing at her theatrics, I closed the door just as Madame Serena stepped out of her shop. "Mary." She rolled the r in my name, though she didn't usually have an accent. Madame Serena dressed the part of a fortuneteller in her multicolored skirt and headband around her hair. She colored her eyelids a dark shade and wore large hoops in her ears. The bangles on her pale-skinned arm clanged as she walked toward me.

"I see you have been playing with the forces of darkness this day," her eyes scanned up and down my form.

I didn't need to look down at myself to know what she meant. The crime scene might have been cold, but the left-over auras of the demons who had been there would cling to me until I took another shower. The officers would probably all experience bad dreams and other misfortunes for a few days until the demonic auras fell off.

"Don't I always?"

"You should be more careful," she tut-tutted, "you never know when those demons might catch you by surprise."

"That's why I carry this as well," opening my jacket slightly, I let her see the Glock 42 sitting in my shoulder holster. I didn't care for guns. In my opinion, they did more harm than good, but after one simple exorcism that had turned into a whole nest of demon-possessed humans, and I had come to carry it with me regardless. Wouldn't stop a demon, but it would slow them down long enough for me to get away.

The Madame gave a short nod and finished pulling the metal bars over her shop front.

"Closing early?" It was barely past ten. Madame Serena usually stayed open until midnight. Said she got more business that way and she had an excuse then not to open until noon.

Madame Serena's eyes shifted around us, "There is evil out this night. Don't you feel it?"

Unlike many psychics who advertised as being the real thing, Madame Serena actually knew what she was talking about, eighty-nine percent of the time. The other eleven percent she couldn't tell you if it was going to rain any more than the weatherman, and not to forget the fact that an angel lived above her. I would think someone who was a hundred percent blessed with the sight would see through me in one second flat.

"It's Los Angeles; the majority of its occupants are up to something evil," I half-heartedly laughed. Sadly, Madame Serena and the rest of the human citizens would never know how true those words were.

I waved a hand at my landlord before making my way up the stairs to my office. As I got to the top of the stairs, I could see the front door was open. Reaching into my jacket, I unsnapped the holster and withdrew my Glock. With my back to the wall, I reached out and pushed the door inward.

The door creaked open, and I slid through the doorway, my gun poised and ready. When nothing immediately jumped out at me I relaxed. I moved to put my gun away figuring Trisha or I had simply forgotten to close the door when, from out of the corner of my eye, I saw a figure jump out at me.

Quick on my feet, I dodged to the side causing the intruder to tumble to the sparsely-carpeted office waiting area. Spinning around, I pulled my gun back out and pointed it toward the figure crouched on the floor. A woman. A crying woman. Her aura didn't come off as demonic, so I lowered my gun but didn't holster it. Humans were crazy, especially emotional ones.

"Excuse me," I started, "but office hours are from nine to six. I'll have to ask you to come back tomorrow."

The woman gave a short laugh and wiped her hand over her face. She moved shakily to her feet, her balance off enough to make me think she had been drinking. Now that I could actually see her, I could tell she wasn't some common thief.

Her brown hair had fallen out of her probably once neat and tidy bun, tears streaked her face and her makeup had begun to run. The light green skirt and business jacket set were definitely not something someone would wear while breaking and entering.

"I apologize for the intrusion," the woman sniffed, embarrassment coloring her voice, "I've always prided myself on being a diplomatic woman, not one who goes on a rampage once they find out their spouse is cheating on them," she moved her hands as she explained, and I still had no idea what she was talking about.

"Was there something I could help you with? If you need evidence against your spouse I could help you with that." The moment the words came out of my mouth I knew it was the wrong thing to say.

The embarrassment on her face was gone and a barely contained rage colored her eyes. "I just bet you could. You gold-digging whore."

Taken aback by her comments, I didn't know what to say. I only knew what a gold-digging whore was because of the silly shows that Trisha sometimes watched while I was around. Why this woman thought I was either, was beyond me.

"I'm not sure I understand you correctly," I slipped my gun into the holster but didn't button it back, just in case, "How am I someone who sleeps with someone on the pretense of getting their money?"

The way I said the phrase clearly confused the woman because her brow crinkled, "You have no idea what I'm talking about, do you?"

"It is that obvious?" I held my hands out to the sides with a small smile. "Let's start over. I'm Mary Wiles, I'm a private detective and you are currently in my office," I held my hand out to her in the customary fashion.

"Alyssa Fredrickson," she took my hand in hers and gave it a firm shake. Not a small one like most women do that don't want to portray themselves as anything other than dainty. It made my respect for her rise.

"Fredrickson?" I asked, the name sounding familiar.

"Yes, as in Donald Fredrickson's wife. The one you are having an affair with," she

48

said it like she wasn't exactly certain that was true now. Which it wasn't. But it did remind me who she was.

Donald, or Donny as he insisted I call him, had come in a few days ago wanting me to follow his wife around. He had found some charges for hotel stays on their credit card and feared she was cheating on him. The guy had been really torn up about it. He had just paid me the retainer fee, but I hadn't actually gotten around to doing it yet with the recent exorcism of Father Dominic and the new case with the police.

"I do know your husband, but I can assure you it is only in a professional manner. In fact," I moved over to Trisha's desk and flicked through the papers there trying to find Donald's file. Once I found it I held it out to her, "he actually came to me about the very same thing."

Alyssa took the folder in her hand and read over the notes of our meeting, "Hotel charges? I thought those were his and then when I saw he had called your number a bunch of times I swore he was the one having the affair!"

I led Alyssa over to the lumpy couch in the waiting area where she flopped down on the cushion, "I don't understand. If I'm not cheating and he's not cheating, then who do the charges belong to?"

She glanced up at me as if I had all the answers. I wanted to say, "Hey don't look at me, I just work here," but I had a feeling that wouldn't go over too well. Instead, I sat down next to her and asked, "Who else has access to your credit card? A friend maybe? Or a housekeeper?"

"We have a teenage son, Jared. But he's such a good boy. Always does his homework, stays the night at his friend, Tom's on Friday's to work on school projects," she said slowly as if what she was saying just took hold and then the rage was back. Jumping to her feet, she waved the folder in the air. "That lying little brat! He's not staying with his friend at all. I thought it was weird that the charges were for Friday nights when Donald and I have our date night those nights and spend the majority of the time together."

"See," I said, hoping to calm her and then get her the heck out of my office, "he wasn't cheating after all."

She turned to me then, tears welling up in her eyes, "I'm so sorry. Here I am attacking you and calling you dreadful names when it was my good-for-nothing son pulling the wool over my eyes. You must think I'm such a horrible person."

I shook my head and patted her on the shoulder, "No, of course not. It's an honest mistake," I took her by the elbow and started to lead her toward the front door, "Now, why don't you go on home and talk to Donald so you can get this all sorted out. Let him know I'll make sure to refund the payment he made as well."

"Oh no!" she turned toward me, "You keep it. After all this, you have definitely earned that money."

"But I didn't really do anything. I hadn't even started the case yet," I argued, though I knew Trisha would kill me. I barely paid her as it was and if I kept not taking payment I wouldn't even have a home to work out of.

"No, I insist. You've saved my marriage. I couldn't possibly take the money back."

Alyssa shook her head, a firm look on her face that told me I was wasting my breath.

"Very well, thank you," I opened the door for her and smiled, "I hope you get everything worked out."

"I will and thank you so much."

I closed the door on the ecstatic wife and heaved a big sigh. Sometimes I would rather just face a horde of demons than deal with the drama of cheating spouses. Sadly, Alyssa Fredrickson was not the first disgruntled spouse that I had encountered, but she was the first to leave with a smile on her face. That was at least saying something.

Locking the door with a snap, I pulled my jacket off and hung it next to the door on the coat hanger. I unsnapped the gun holster and let it hang loose as I moved into my bedroom-slash-office. Making sure no one else was going to jump out at me, I worked on taking my boots and clothing off. Not only did I have demon to wash off, but also the sickly sweet perfume Alyssa had been wearing.

I tried to make my shower quick, not wanting it to be after midnight before I finally got to bed, but who was I kidding.

Taking showers was one of the luxuries on earth that I actually appreciated. In heaven, dirt didn't really exist, and so there was no need to bathe at all. Now, I didn't know how I'd live without it.

By the time I got out of the shower and into bed it was just after midnight. No sooner had I closed my eyes when my phone went off.

Scrambling around for it in the dark, I glanced at the red digits on the night stand. Four thirty. I'd have less than five hours of sleep. Yay.

Picking up the phone, I pressed it to my ear. "Hello?"

"Mary? Did I wake you?" Thompson's voice asked on the other line.

"Only vampires are awake at this time of day, Randall. You better make it good," safe to say I was not a happy sleep-deprived angel.

"Vampires? Those exist too?" the eagerness in his voice almost made me smile. Almost.

"It was an example, Thompson. What do you want?" I all but growled into the phone.

He paused for a moment and then cleared his throat, "Oh, well, we have a lead. The woman's name was Emily Green. She, and the past two victims, were all recent patrons of the same bar before their mysterious disappearances. We want you to go down there and check it out. See what kind of information you can get."

"Why me? Can't one of your officers do it?" I leaned up on my elbow, my eyes catching the clock again, and the urge to chuck it across the room filled me. Note to self: turn off the phone before going to bed.

"Yeah, but well, it's one of your kind of bars," he paused for a moment, "plus you're prettier than any of my guys. If we are catching a woman-killer it's best to send in a woman, right?"

"Thanks, Thompson," I half laughed at his backhanded way of giving me a compliment, "So, what bar is it?"

"Actually, you are in luck. It just so happens to be your boyfriend's bar. The Night Owl," Thompson said, the humor clear in his voice.

"He's not my boyfriend," I stated simply as if I was commenting on the weather.

Thompson laughed, "Whatever you say, Wiles. You just get down there and work your magic before another body shows up," his tone turned serious at the potential of another murder.

Neither one of us were laughing as I hung up the phone. Thompson might act like he knew how likely another body showing up would be but from my experience with demons, it wasn't a possibility, it was a certainty. There was always another body.

5

THE NIGHT OWL WAS one of L.A.'s best-kept secrets and for good reason. Not only was it away from the tourist areas but it was a local hang-out for those of the supernatural persuasion.

Not that Thompson knew that when he'd sent me down here. But the fact that the victims had last been seen here just helped solidify my previous judgment. The murders were definitely demon-related.

The Night Owl was not a hole in the wall. The dark mahogany wood door to the bar creaked open and closed behind me without help. The bar front had two windows, both blacked out so that the lighting could be decided by the owner, who kept it at a dim ambient setting.

I'd commented before about how the bar practically screamed paranormal and general naughtiness. Not just because of the lighting but the music seemed to always have a sultry beat that reverberated through me every step I took. Almost like the bar itself was trying to seduce me.

As I let my eyes adjust to the bar's dim lighting, I realized that I probably wasn't far from the truth. Those who came to The Night Owl rarely left alone, and more often than not, there were various couples completely absorbed in each other. So much so that sometimes they became a bit freer with their kisses and their hands roamed more than would be seen appropriate in most human's eyes.

My gaze landed on a couple on the dance floor. They were the only ones in the middle of the small space but they didn't seem to mind. The male had one hand cupping the woman's backside. His fingers dug into the fleshy bits through her short dress, causing it to rise slightly and almost flash the room.

The woman had a leg hooked around her partner's hip and was grinding herself against the thigh between her legs. Her head was thrown back, her hair cascading down her back as she opened her mouth in a silent cry of pleasure. If anyone cared about the couple practically dry humping in the middle of the room no one said anything or even looked up from their drinks.

"Have you been waiting long?"

The husky tone of the owner's voice made me smile. Turning toward the bar's owner, I said, "Not at all."

Sidney Magnus, Sid to his friends, stood just an inch above me making it easy to meet his amused gaze. Even shadowed by the bar's lighting, I could still make out the gold that created a ring around his green eyes. Though human as could be, the glow of them mesmerized me in such a way that I had thought more than once he had to be more than what he seemed.

But thankfully, the only thing that lay beneath the dark t-shirts he always sported were bulging biceps and abs I had a strange urge to lick. I shook my head and credited the desire to the bar getting to me.

I forced my attention back up to his eyes and found him watching me, a curious tilt to his head. "What's on your mind, angel?"

I frowned at the nickname. Stepping up to the bar, I slid onto a stool before him. "Don't call me that," I said in a hushed tone while casting a sideways glance at the other patrons.

Sid leaned forward on the bar, his face a foot from mine as he whispered back, "Why? Afraid someone might try and take you on?"

Not rising to his bait, I waved him off. "You know that's not why."

The only time I came to The Night Owl was when I needed information. If everyone in the place knew I was an angel, even if they thought I was a fallen one, they'd close up tighter than a nun's habit. It also made my need to exorcise any demon I saw on sight hard to control. I couldn't blow my cover because of my hatred toward the clientele.

"Then why come here?" Sid asked pretending to wipe down the bar though we both knew it was spotless. Sid might look like the rugged bad boy who wanted nothing more than to get down and dirty, but anyone who really knew him knew he

59

ran a tight ship. Dirt wouldn't dare cross his threshold.

"Maybe I just like your company."

"We both know that's not it," he gave a bitter laugh.

My brows creased and I frowned harder. There was something off about him today. Usually, he was all smiles and flirting, his eyes practically undressing me every time we met. But today he hadn't even glanced lower than my chin. Not that my jeans and polo shirt were anything to write home about, but still it was odd.

"What's wrong?"

"Why would something be wrong?" he practically growled before sighing. He ran a hand through his dark, almost black hair and the rosary he wore wrapped around his wrist came unwound letting the cross swing in the air. A few of the bar's occupants relocated at the sight while one hissed at Sid, he glared in return before turning his eyes back to me.

"Why do you wear it, if it just pisses your customers off?" Ignoring the way he had answered me, I gestured at the rosary as he wrapped it back around his wrist. If he wanted to be in a mood, then who was I to argue?

"Let's just say you wouldn't like me without it." His eyes darkened for a moment before he gave me a lopsided grin. That look made my stomach do funny things that almost distracted me from his ominous answer. *Worry about it later, Mary. You're here for a reason.*

Listening to my own advice for once, I dug into the back pocket of my jeans and set out the pictures of the three victims so far. Thompson had had someone send them over to the office earlier today, saying it might help get me some answers. Here's hoping he was right.

"You're right, though. I'm not here to see you. Have you seen her?" I tapped the image of the first victim, a blonde who was more girl than woman. She couldn't have been more than eighteen, poor thing. How had she gotten mixed up with demons?

Sid picked the picture up, squinting at it in the light. The bar probably wasn't the place to be questioning him about the victims. If he had seen any of them, it would be hard to recognize your own mother in the dark corners of the bar let alone a complete stranger. It was safe to say I didn't have high hopes.

"Yeah, I've seen her."

Sid's answer made me pause. "You have?"

"Yeah," he nodded and then tapped his fingers on the other two images on the bar top, "these two, too."

Thompson had also sent over the coroner's report for all the victims. The second and third victims were both young and had no similar qualities. The only thing they could discern from their bodies and families was that they had been good girls. So much so that the thought that they would give their virginity to a group rather than when they got married had been unthinkable. Problem was, if being a virgin was the only criteria the demons we were going for, we were screwed.

"When did you see them last? Were they with anyone?" the questions spewed out of me but Sid wasn't listening. His eyes kept flickering from me to the couple on the dance floor.

I glanced over my shoulder to the pair who were no longer pretending to dance; they were practically ripping each other's clothes off. The other customers had begun to notice now all attempts at pretense was gone.

I raised an eyebrow at Sid and said, "Some people, right?"

The joke fell flat as Sid's gaze turned back to me, a storm of emotion in his eyes. There was definitely something off about him today.

Reading someone's soul wasn't something I could just turn off and on as I liked. I had to consciously focus on their physical being, so flipping over was as easy as breathing for me.

But when I let that control go and focused on Sid's, what I saw surprised me. Murky. That's the only color I could describe it. The first time I meet someone I always read their soul to get an idea of what kind of person they are, the same went for Sid. His soul had always been an off white, verging on pristine but the thick grayish tint that was going on today was not like him at all. Neither was the way he was acting.

His hands gripped the counter like he was forcing himself to stay behind the bar. His jaw muscle flexed, his hazel eyes now more brown than green. Something had him freaked out. But what?

"Sid?" I started, but he cut me off, his gaze jerking from the couple back to me.

"What?" he snapped. He gathered up the photos on the bar and thrust them at me. "Here, the guy I saw them with is over there," Sid gestured violently at the corner where a lone figure sat in the near dark.

I turned back to Sid to thank him but he was already storming around the bar and toward the couple on the dance floor. The woman's dress had been unzipped and drawn halfway down her body, showing anyone behind her she wasn't wearing a bra. The man's face was buried in her neck and they clung to each other. Making my way through the bar, I half watched the scene unfold as Sid approached them.

He didn't jerk them apart or yell at them. Instead, he murmured in the man's ear for a moment and then gestured toward the bar area. The man smiled and nodded before helping his partner cover back up. Sid led the two across the bar and through a door that I knew led to the back office.

Instead of closing the two of them in there, to what I could only assume was to finish what they started, Sid followed them in, the door shutting tight behind him. My brow furrowed. Odd.

Before I could convince myself to not follow after him and figure out what was going on, my phone chirped. Trisha had texted me.

The symbols you gave me were demonic all right.

Yeah? I texted back.

I didn't have long to wait before she messaged me again with an image of a demon who had horns on more than just his head.

Asmodeus, demon of lust. At least if you believe the Catholics.

Before I could respond back she sent me another.

All I can say is — ouch!

I smiled slightly at her last comment. I could just see the disgust on her face as she sent that text. Little did she know that the images humans drew of demons and angels were rarely what they truly looked like. I should know.

Good work. I'll check in when I'm done here, I shot back before tucking my phone back into my jacket pocket. Tossing a frown at the office door once more, I made for the table Sid had so rudely pointed out.

Let Sid have his secrets. I had a murder to solve and demons to exorcise.

"Hey, sweetheart, can I help you?" the man said before I even stopped in front of the table. Beady eyes leered at me as he gave me a greasy smile. I didn't need to look into this guy's soul to know he was possessed. His pores oozed evil. Either the demon was too low-level to conceal himself or he generally didn't give a crap.

"Mind if I sit here?" Easing down into the seat across from him, I gave him as much attention as he was giving me. Even if he hadn't been possessed the guy still would have rated on Trisha's sleazy scale.

Loud clothes? My eyes zeroed in on the red and black patterned silk shirt that hung off his lanky frame. Check. Balding but trying to hide it behind a toupee or hat? The guy smoothed a hand over the hair he had combed over to try to hide the bare skin at the top of his head. I made a face. Close enough.

If those attributes didn't qualify him for the sleaze box, then the way his eyes repeatedly drifted to my breasts definitely did. Demons. I had the urge to roll my eyes but kept it in check.

He licked his lips before his eyes flicked back up to my face, smiling. "Well, you know I was saving that spot for my friend but he's not near as pretty as you." He scrubbed a thumb over his nose, his eyes once more finding my chest.

"Aren't you sweet?" I gave a tight smile. *You need him alive, Mary*, I reminded myself. "What's your name?"

"Martin," his hands reached across the table where I had rested mine, and I forced myself not to pull away as he placed his cool fingertips on top of mine, "So, what's a beautiful thing like you doing here all by yourself?" he glanced around as if searching for someone, "You're not that bartender's girl, are you?"

"No. I'm not with him."

"Good. Cause," Martin stroked the top of my hand and leaned toward me, "between you and me," he said in a hushed voice, "he's nothing but bottom-feeder trash. Not worth more than a soul suck."

Before he could finish the last word, I had my hands out from under his and his face smashed into the table top.

"What the fuck, lady?" he screamed causing the other patrons to look our way briefly before turning back to their drinks. *Yeah, that's right mind your own business.*

"I was going to be nice about this," I growled in his ear, my anger beating down on me, "but since you decided to insult my friend, I'm not feeling so giving," I jerked the image of the latest victim from my pocket and shoved it into his face, "What did you do to her?"

The guy's eyes widened and he tried to shake his head against my grip on his face. "I haven't seen her before. I swear!"

"Oh really? Are you sure?" I pressed down harder on the side of his face, a whimper coming from his throat.

"I'm sure! I'm sure. I've never seen her."

"Fine," I grabbed him by the back of his shirt and dragged him out of his chair. Tossing a glare at the curious customers, I pulled him over to where the restroom door was and shoved him inside.

Checking that we were alone, I closed the door and locked it. Martin shook in my grip but didn't try to get away anymore. The demon in him must be some lower-level bottom-feeder like he tried to accuse Sid of being. Otherwise, he'd have put up more of a fight. I'd feel sorry for him if I wasn't so enraged.

Over the last five years, I had learned to embrace the emotions that came from losing my wings. Pain. Sadness. Rage. I had felt all of these over the course of my time on earth, each and every one of them new to a once pure and unhindered angel. Why should I ever worry or feel pain? I was in the presence of my creator. Nothing else mattered but him. Boy, was I wrong.

I reached into my pocket and pulled out my charm. The moment Martin's eyes landed on it, he twisted in my grip. Hissing at me, the demon in him fully came to the surface. "No! Leave us. Leave us."

"You should have thought of that before you started raping and killing virgins, asshole," I spit out, pushing him against the bathroom wall. I didn't curse often, didn't really see the point, but I'd been told by many that sometimes regular words just didn't cut it. In this case, it couldn't be truer. There wasn't a word bad enough for his kind.

The demon in Martin made his eyes widen, and his mouth dropped open as he shook his head, "We killed no one! We just get the girls, we don't do anything to them. We swear!"

"Is that so?" I held the charm in my hand like a threat.

His dark eyes stared at the charm as he squealed, "Yes! We go through a site. They want young girls looking for love. It's easy enough to find those who are untouched."

Frowning at his answer, I gave him a little shake, "What site?"

"Guy f-for you. Now let us go. We did nothing!" Martin fought against my grip hard enough I had to actually put some effort into it.

"Oh, but you did," I allowed the chain of the charm to drop into the palm of my hand, "You might not have killed those girls personally but there is something you did do."

"What?"

"You existed," I shoved the charm onto his forehead. The demon inside of Martin screamed. Darkness poured out of every orifice and sank into the floor until Martin's eyes cleared to a light blue. Before I could open my mouth to explain, his eyes fluttered closed and he passed out.

I looked down at his crumpled form and then shrugged. Someone would find him eventually. I unlocked the door and pushed it open, forcing Martin to move further into the bathroom. I didn't have time to coddle him. There were others who needed my help more. If I got there in time.

6

TRISHA PICKED ME UP from the bar and took me to the West L.A. Police Department. Since it was after office hours, Trisha's mother wasn't exactly happy that I'd called.

But what could I do? Calling a taxi wasn't in my budget, especially not in L.A. Not on my shitty salary.

I could give in and learn to drive, but the last time I'd tried I'd had a panic attack. Who knew driving a car could remind you so much of flying? Not me.

"Want me to wait here?" Trisha called out the window.

I glanced back at Trisha, whose black hair was twisted into some kind of bun on either side of her head, multicolored extensions coming from the middle. It reminded me of those party poppers that shot out streamers and confetti.

I shook my head, "No. You go on home. Who knows how long this might take. I'll make Thompson take me."

Her nose crinkled slightly making her heavily outlined eyes squint. "Are you sure you want to do that? I mean ride with the man and all?"

I smirked. "I already work for them hard to fall much further."

"You got it boss." she gave me a thumbs-up before putting the car in gear and then peeling out of the police station parking lot.

That girl.

I smiled and shook my head as I walked through the doorway of the West L.A. Police Station. The receptionist glanced up from her paperwork briefly before buzzing me in. Thankfully, I'd been here often enough not to need to explain myself. It'd be a pain to have to do it every time.

I hadn't set more than one foot into the office area of the precinct when Thompson called my name.

"Wiles! Get in here," the sergeant's head popped out of one of the doorways along the hall before disappearing back inside.

Maneuvering between the desks, I tried to ignore the glares stabbing into my back. When you are an angel, even a seemingly-fallen angel, one of the places you didn't want to be was in a police station.

The majority of those who come into the police station are good. For the most part. But there were people whose souls were so dark that even a demon wouldn't want to be housed within them. Those humans, for some reason or another, could just sense what I am. They don't know exactly what it is about me, but just my presence makes their insides recoil. As if I might smite them on the spot. I know because the first time I'd come to the precinct I'd had to knock one of them out before he'd shot me with his stolen gun.

I sighed and rounded my shoulders, determined to ignore the feeling. The only place I could think of that could be worse would be a prison. Even the thought of it made me shiver.

Stepping into the room, my eyes immediately went to the one-way mirror looking into one of the interrogation rooms. Sitting at the metal table was a man—dirty blonde hair and a lanky build, he couldn't have been more than thirty. His face was pinched and his gaze hard and focused on the surface of the table in front of him. Only one emotion emanated from him. Worry.

"Coffee?"

My eyes jerked from the man to Thompson who stood by the coffee pot in what had to be yesterday's clothes based on how wrinkled and worn they were. The pot of dark liquid he held in his hand made me curl my lip in disgust.

I'd learned the hard way that coffee and I didn't really get along. The one and only time I'd ever had the bitter drink my senses had gone on overdrive.

Everywhere I'd looked I'd seen demons. The dark auras around me had tripled in size. Thankfully, I hadn't had my gun at the time or someone might have gotten hurt. It hadn't lasted long though, my metabolism being faster than a human's so it was out of my system within ten minutes, but I had sworn never again.

Alcohol was something else I was wary of, but that was a whole different matter.

"No thanks," I replied and then I nodded toward the man, "What's up with him?"

Thompson looked up from the cup of coffee he was drowning in sugar and creamer and stared at the mirror. "Bill Harold. He's the ex-boyfriend and our only suspect in the murder of Amelia Johnson. The guy was caught with the murder weapon in his suitcase," he gave a disgusted scoff, wiping hand on his shirt, "Doesn't even have the decency to confess."

"I wouldn't either if I was innocent," I crossed my arms over my chest and stared at the man. My gaze shifted over to his soul. Almost as white as a newborn babe's. If this guy had ever even lied in his life, I'd eat my shoe.

"You don't think he did it?"

Pointing at Bill, I said with confidence, "I know he didn't."

"How do you know?" Thompson's fuzzy eyebrows scrunched down.

"How do I know any of the things I know?" I shrugged and said, "Experience."

Thompson took a sip of his coffee which caused him to grimace, and then said, "I'm going to need more than that to get him off the hook. Like someone else to look into."

"Sorry, Sergeant can't give you that. I'm not psychic."

Then what are you? I could see the question form on Thompson's lips but instead of saying it, he shook his head and turned his attention back to the file he had on a table in the small room.

Just then a detective I hadn't met before, poked his head into the room. "Hey Serg, what did you want to do with Harold? He's been sweating it out for most of the day now."

My eyes narrowed on Thompson, "You've made that poor man wait all day? What'd you think? He would just suddenly change his story?" I didn't even try to hide the utter disgust in my voice.

Thompson glanced to the detective and then back to me before saying, "Let the guy go. He's not our man."

"But Sergeant, are you sure? We found him with the murder weapon. We can't just let him go without another lead."

"Are you questioning me, Barkley?" Thompson snapped.

The detective opened his mouth, but then closed it and shook his head, "No sir. I'll get the paperwork started, sir."

When the detective closed the door behind him, Thompson, asked, "So what did you find out?"

The change of topic didn't surprise me. Most people didn't want to admit when they were wrong. Pride has always been one of humanity's greatest downfalls. Angels it seemed, too.

Not prodding any further into his decisions, I leaned against the desk and sighed, "Well, there is good news and bad news."

"Bad news? What bad news?" Thompson frowned.

I scratched the side of my face and gave a little laugh, "You see I kind of exorcised the demon possessing the guy."

"So? Bring the guy in. We can question him."

I shook my head, "Sadly it doesn't work that way. Most people who are possessed are lucky to still be alive when the demon is removed. The likelihood of him knowing anything that had happened during possession is close to none."

Watching Thompson's face change from confused to enraged was a curious sight. His skin paled as if he might be sick and then a shudder went through him. Then, almost like magic, the paleness of his skin morphed into a purplish red. I feared the blood vessels in his eyes might pop from the way they bulged out of their sockets.

"So," he heaved, "you're telling me that the one suspect we had to solve this case was in the palm of your hands and instead of bringing him in for questioning, you exorcised his ass? Is that what you're telling me?" There was a threat in his voice as if he was hoping I would change my story, but it didn't do any good.

"Yeah, pretty much," I shrugged.

"What the hell do I even keep you around for?" he roared at me, spittle spraying across my face. Grimacing, I wiped the back of my jacket-sleeve across my cheeks and forehead.

Blech.

Thompson didn't give me a chance to answer his question before he continued rampaging.

"Do you know what you've done?" he shook a finger at me, "You've jeopardized this whole case. Now, we'll never know where they're grabbing the girls from or how to even stop them," Thompson paused his chest heaving as he pulled in lungfuls of air. When he had caught his breath, his voice lowered but no less enraged, "You said yourself there'd be more murders. Now, those lives are on you," he pointed a finger at me.

Thompson's outburst wasn't anything new. He could be cool and collected one minute but the moment you screw up his investigation he would jump down your throat. This wasn't the first time I'd gotten yelled at and probably wouldn't be the last.

I raised a brow at him, waiting, "Are you done?"

Apparently, those were not the right words to say in this instance because his fingers curled into a fist and for a second I thought he might hit me. But he seemed to think better of it and dropped his hand with a sigh, "Just get out."

He turned his back on me and most people would have taken that as a dismissal. But I wasn't most people.

"So, as I was saying, there is bad news," Thompson spun on his heel his mouth open, probably to yell at me again, but I held a hand up and said, "*and* good news."

I paused for a moment to make sure he wasn't going to explode on me again before I said, "The bad news is yes, the demon is gone. The good news is that there will be another."

"How do you know?"

"There's always another one," like roaches, they were.

"Okay," Thompson drew out, "so this time instead of taking him on yourself, bring him in so we can interrogate him."

I snorted, "He won't tell you anything."

"If he knows what's good for him, he will," Thompson crossed his arms over his chest, puffing it out, the alpha male seeking attention.

"Do you think they care?" I pushed off the table. "Look, *you* know humans. I know demons. And let me just tell you, that your little weapon there," I pointed to his gun holster, "won't do anything but piss them off."

"Then we'll arrest them for obstruction of justice."

"And what then?" I asked, "They'll just find some other body to possess, leaving you with a confused and possibly dead suspect."

Thompson opened his mouth and then shut it. After a moment, he growled, "Well then there is no good news. Cause either way we are fucked!" he threw his hands up in the air.

"Not exactly," I stopped him from going further, "I didn't just exorcise the guy without getting some information out of him."

"You didn't?" he dropped his hands with an almost-hopeful gleam in his eyes.

I nodded, "They are getting the girls from a site called *Guy for You*. Heard of it?"

Thompson's brow furrowed and then he marched over to the door. Jerking it open, he hollered, "Wiltberger! Get in here."

A few seconds later a beefy guy with glasses carrying a laptop, stumbled in.

"What's up, Sergeant?" when his eyes landed on me, he smiled, "Oh, hey Mary."

Wiltberger was the resident brain. He was to the precinct what Trisha was to me. I'd met him a few times before but he usually kept to himself.

I gave him a small wave before Thompson jumped in, "Have you heard of a site called *Guy for You*?"

Wiltberger pushed his glasses up his nose and typed a few things on his computer. Turning the screen around, he showed up a website decorated int black and red. "The site is actually called Guy 4 U, with the number four and the letter u instead of the word 'you'."

"That's great and all Wiltberger, but what is it?" Thompson glared down at the screen.

"It's a dating site," Wiltberger was unaffected by the Sergeant's short temper. Guess I wasn't the only one who was used to Thompson's rage.

The moment the words came out of Wiltburger's mouth though, Thompson's expression changed. A slow creepy smile crept up his face and then his eyes locked on me.

Why was he staring at me like that?

Then it dawned on me.

"No."

"Yes," Thompson argued stepping around Wiltberger to stop in front of me.

"No." I shook my head this time my hands on my hips. I was not backing down on this.

"You fucked up, so you get to fix it."

"How is me signing up for a dating site going to fix it?" I gestured at the computer, ignoring how Wiltberger was smiling at us.

"You go undercover. Pretend to be some innocent girl looking for love." Just the way he said the words was insulting. "Then they'll snatch you up not knowing any better."

"It'll be great," Wiltberger jumped in, "I'd help you set up your profile but they want you to go to their headquarters for an interview first. It's all very standard procedure nowadays. They don't want to sign up any wackos."

"Great," I forced a smile.

"Good," Thompson slapped me on the back, "then it's all settled. You better go find yourself something nice to wear. You've got a date with destiny."

Thompson followed Wiltberger out of the room before I could tell him I had in no way agreed to this.

"But I've never been on a date."

7

"I DON'T UNDERSTAND WHY I can't just hack into the site and set up a profile? I mean do you really need to go to all this hassle?" Trisha asked, flipping through the clothes in my closet at the office.

"Because we need to make sure the headquarters of Guy 4 U isn't helping the demons," I said from my desk.

"Well, I can't believe you don't own a dress," Trisha picked up one of my t-shirts before making a face and tossing it on the ever-growing pile of rejects on the floor.

Ever since I'd told her about my new undercover role she had insisted on helping me dress for the interview. I didn't see why I couldn't just wear what I normally wore, but just suggesting that made her go off on a tangent.

"I've never needed one," I said from my desk. I clicked the mouse on the About page of the Guy 4 U site. If I was going undercover I had find out everything I needed to know about them.

"That, I can't believe."

"Why not?" I glanced up from the computer.

Trisha turned from the minuscule closet with her hands on her hips. "Are you kidding me? You're a total hottie. If I played for the other team, I'd totally do you."

"Uh, thanks?" I didn't know what team she was talking about but I'd learned it was best to just nod and smile when it came to Trisha.

"Come on," Trisha whined. "You are what? Twenty-six?"

"Something like that," I muttered. I couldn't very well tell her I was more than a millennia old in human years. Weirdly enough, by angel standards, I landed in the age range the humans go by, though I didn't behave even close to how most humans believed I should. A fact that Trisha constantly reminded me of.

"I'm just saying, you have the bod, you have a sweet job. You should be getting out there. Shaking your groove thing," she lifted her hands above her head and swiveled her hips.

I frowned.

Throwing her hands up the in air, Trisha let out an exasperated growl. "Come on. Work with me here. What do you normally wear on dates? Because, not to overstep my bounds," she held her hands up in front of her and then pointed a thumb back to my closet, "but unless you are looking to get jiggy with a biker gang, you've got no suitable date clothes."

"What is suitable date clothes?" I raised a brow at her.

"You know. Dresses. Short skirts. Maybe even something that shows off the girls," she adjusted her top around her breasts.

"Oh."

At my one-word answer, Trisha's lips twisted downward, "I'm starting to think you don't know what I mean," When I didn't answer she made a small dramatic gasp.

Stomping over to where I sat, she slammed her hands down on the desk in front of me. "You've never been on a date before, have you?"

I turned my eyes back to the screen and shrugged, "No, not really."

"Not really? Is that like you Netflix and chill? 'Cause girl, you are worth more than that," she pursed her darkly made-up lips together and snapped her fingers.

"Netflix and chill? Is that like with ice cream or something?"

"No, it's like you watch Netflix with a guy under the pretense that you are on a date when you both know it's just about getting laid."

"You mean have intercourse."

"Yes, I mean intercourse," she rolled her eyes.

I smiled, happy to actually know one thing she was talking about. I really needed to pay more attention to Trisha when she was talking.

"Well," Trisha leaned off the desk and crossed her arms, "I hate to break it to you, boss, but you don't own anything that will make these guys think you are a virgin ripe for the sacrificing."

"So what do you propose I do?"

Trisha gave a slow creepy smile, "It means we have to go shopping."

TWO HOURS AND WAY more stores than I could count later, Trisha and I stumbled back through my office door.

Collapsing on the waiting-area couch, I watched as Trish thumbed through the bags of clothing she had insisted I buy. I'd told her I didn't exactly have shopping money but she simply lifted a black credit card and said, "I've gotcha covered. Lifted it off my old woman. We'll just bill the Sergeant for it."

Now, though, I felt like she was more interested in the chance to play dress up with me than to get clothes for work.

"So what do you think?" Trisha held up a white sun dress that I remembered had spun around my knees when I'd worn it. "Nice girl enough?"

"Sure," I shrugged not having any idea why wearing a certain type of clothing qualified one as a nice girl. Either they were or they weren't, wearing a specific kind of clothes wouldn't change that.

Standing from the couch, I took the dress from Trisha and started to strip. I hadn't gotten more than just my shirt off before Trisha cleared her throat.

"What?" I looked at Trisha standing only in my bra and jeans. She pressed her lips tight together before pointing toward the door.

Spinning around, my eyes locked on Thompson standing in the doorway of the office. "Hey Sergeant, we're about ready."

Thompson seemed stunned for a moment, staring at me, and then he shook his head. His face colored red and he stared hard at the ceiling as he said, "I can see that. Do you make a habit of changing in your waiting area?"

Pulling the dress over my head, I shimmied out of my jeans. "No. Not really. Did you come here for something, Thompson?"

"Oh, yeah," Thompson coughed and looked at me out of the corner of his eye until he was satisfied that I was clothed. "I just wanted to give you this," he held out a black case.

"What's this?" I took the case and unzipped it. Inside was some sort of corded device.

"It's a wire," Trisha stated stepping up next to me, "You wear it and they can hear everything is going on."

"This way you can't mess up again," Thompson said.

I glared at him, "No."

"No?" Thompson asked, his tone disbelieving. "What do you mean no? You don't really have a choice in the matter. You've already fucked up by exorcising our only suspect. You're lucky the higher-ups are even letting you do this."

That made me angry but before I could get a word out Trisha jumped in, "Letting her? Letting her? She's the one helping you!"

"Trisha," I began but she cut me off with a wave of her hand.

"No! This guy needs to know who the one doing him a favor is. She doesn't have to do shit for you. You can get one of your police girls to sign up to be sacrificed. We have adulterous spouses to catch," she snapped her fingers in front of

Thompson's face before grabbing my arm and dragging me toward my office door.

"Fine. Fine," Thompson called out before we could get out of the room, "I'm sorry. You don't have to wear the wire if you don't want to but," he pointed a finger at me as he looked me in the eye, "if you mess up again I won't be able to save your butt. You'll be relying on those naughty pictures to pay your bills."

"When they pay," Trisha commented under her breath but I heard her and nudged her.

"Alright," Thompson tugged up his pants, "what's the alias you are going to go by?"

"Alias?"

Trisha placed a hand on my arm, "Don't worry, boss, I've got this one."

* * *

APPARENTLY, WHEN GOING UNDERCOVER one couldn't use their real name in case the person has heard of you or does a background check. Not that I was worried about them doing a background check on me. There wasn't anything to find.

"If they find out you're a P.I. they might split," Trisha said, following alongside me into the Guy 4 U headquarters.

"Got it," I glanced around the area. For a dating service, it seems too clean. Like more of a hospital than somewhere to find love.

As we approached the door the receptionist had directed us to by, I balanced in my new shoes and tried not to fall on my face.

"Why did I have to wear these again?" I looked down at the white four-inch heeled shoes. "I'm not going to be able to run in these."

Trisha snorted, "Just because you're playing a good girl doesn't mean you can't have fabulous shoes. Besides, they make your butt look great."

I glanced over my shoulder in an attempt to see what she was talking about but I couldn't tell. "I'll just have to take your word for it."

Just then, a tall thin man came out of the office. He smoothed a hand over light straw-colored hair that was slicked back from his face and when his eyes landed on us they lit up.

"Ladies!" he extended a hand out to us, "So happy to have you here with us."

"The pleasure is ours," Trisha grabbed his hand in hers giving it an over enthusiastic shake.

Trisha decided to play undercover as well. Gone were the hot pink extensions, tight corset, and dark makeup, in their place was a red floral printed dress that reached just above her knees and sensible white pumps. With her hair flowing freely down her back, she looked the very definition of wholesome.

"Hello," I shook his hand with minimal enthusiasm. Trisha shot me a look before turning back to the man.

"Don't mind my sister, she's a bit shy. This is her first time signing up for anything like this," Trisha laughed and smiled like she was made for this part. Her ability to swap her personality so fast made me wonder which Trisha was the real one. Have I ever even met her before?

Before I could think too much on it, the man was ushering us inside his office. The walls were made of glass, so if there were any illicit deals with demons going on then everyone would have known about it. His office was much nicer than mine. The great oak desk filled up most of the room and the only solid wall was covered in a large bookshelf.

"Sit, sit," he gestured to the two seats in front of his desk as he took the high-backed one behind it. "As you know, I'm Walter Malark, owner, and founder of Guy 4 U. Where we will make all your dreams come true."

I gave him a tight smile.

I didn't really care for his sales pitch. My dreams were full of screams and carnage. Not something I particularly wanted to come to life. Once was enough.

Not too dissuaded by my off putting demeanor, he continued with a grin, "So tell me about yourselves, ladies. Are you both interested in signing up for the site?" he pointed two fingers at Trisha and me.

"No," I jumped in before Trisha could answer. I didn't need her in any deeper than she already was. "Just me."

"Good. Good. So then. You know who I am, but let's talk about you," he pulled out a pen, clicking the end soundly, "Let's start with the basics. What's your name?"

"Mary," I said.

At the same time that Trisha said, "Marcella."

Walter glanced up from the paper on his desk confusion on his face but Trisha quickly came to the rescue. "Marcella is her legal name but she prefers to go by Mary. She's always thought it was too old-fashioned." Her face pinched as she waved a hand at him.

"Understood," nodding once, he scribbled the name down, "and how old are you Mary?"

"Twenty-six." At least that's why my driver's license said.

"Occupation?"

"Religious counselor."

"Really?" Walter looked up from his desk his eyebrows raised.

"Yes," I nodded and then when he didn't continue with his questions, I added, "I work with troubled teens mostly."

"That's great," he smiled a full-toothed grin as if he was overly pleased with my answer.

Lying wasn't something I really understood. What was the point? Either they were going to like what you say or not. There was no sure-fire way of knowing how someone will react, so lying seemed like a waste of time.

The LAPD and Trisha didn't seem to think that Walter, or any potential dates, would take kindly to a Private Investigator-slash-exorcist. Not that I could blame them. My job screamed run-the-other-way not tell-me-all-your-secrets.

"Alright," Walter clapped his hands and then rubbed them together before getting up from his seat. "Now to the video portion."

"Video?" I glanced at Trisha who just shrugged.

"Yes. All applicants have to do a video." He pulled out a laptop and set up a ball-shaped device with a lens on it.

"Why?"

"It gives the other applicants a better feel for who you are as a person," he answered me and then, when I still gave him a blank look, added, "anyone can write down whatever they want on paper, or online, but we find that video makes it easier to weed out the . . ." he paused for a moment, "undesirables, so to speak."

"Uh, okay," I gave Trisha an uncertain look, my hands clenching and unclenching at my sides.

"Psst," Trisha not so discreetly motioned for me to lean over.

"What?" I whispered, though Walter probably could hear everything we were saying.

"You okay?"

"I'm fine. I didn't expect to be recorded is all."

"It's totally normal," Trisha tried to assure me, "Just hone your inner virgin and you'll be golden."

I chewed on my lip at her words.

"What is it, Mare?" Trisha prodded me, but I looked away.

"Nothing," I shook my head and gave her a weak smile, "just nervous."

I couldn't really tell her what I was thinking. If she thought my never having gone on a date was crazy, then she'd really get a kick out of knowing I'd never had intercourse before.

"All set," Walter thankfully announced before Trisha could ask any more.

"So, I'm going to ask you a series of questions and I just want you to answer as honestly as possible. Can you do that Mary?"

I took a deep breath in and then let it out and gave him a small smile, "Yeah, I can do that."

"Alright, first question. Why did you decide to sign up for a dating site? No luck in the outside world?"

I frowned at his question. For an owner of said dating site, he was coming off pretty judgmental of those who use his page.

"I've found it hard to find others like myself."

"Like other religious people?" Walter asked.

"Not religious," I shook my head and then stared down at my hands. I hoped I looked demure, but really I felt like a fool.

"Do you mean different physically?" Walter coaxed and my eyes snapped up to meet his. They were even more excited than before, making me wonder if this guy really was in line with the demons taking women. Just because he didn't seem possessed didn't mean that he hadn't made a deal with one. A powerful demon could easily pass for human without me knowing. I was good but not that good.

"Yes," I cleared my throat, "I have a hard time finding others like me because many see it as a negative," I sat up straighter as I got into the role, "I'm hoping that you can help me find someone who can appreciate what I am and what I have to give. Do you think you can do that for me?"

I let the hopefulness fill my voice and could almost see Walter rubbing his hands together like he had just hit the jackpot. Too bad for him, he didn't know how wrong he was.

8

THREE DAYS. IT HAD been three days since I had dressed in that getup and applied to have all my dreams come true.

A fat lot of good that did. I readjusted in my seat on the top of fire escape of the building across from my most recent client's spouse's work.

Mrs. Miller believed that her husband was having an affair with his secretary. It was so cliché I had to force myself not to roll my eyes as she explained it to me. It was the same old scenario as I'd heard a thousand times.

They've been working late. They didn't pay them any attention anymore. Worse was when they brought in evidence that they were cheating. I have a special bag in the bottom drawer of my desk that I have collected dirty undergarments from clients over the last few years. I keep meaning to toss them out but somehow it always gets overlooked.

I couldn't even imagine what would happen if Trisha were to find the stash one day. The last thing I needed was for her to think I'm some kind of pervert. Not like this guy.

I clicked the button on the camera in my hand at the middle-aged man who had just appeared in the window. Mr. Miller was indeed having an affair but it wasn't with his secretary—who I had already written off because she was practically graying and the likelihood that he was going for someone older than him was not high.

No, Mr. Miller's tastes ran more on the younger, more muscular side. Someone like his twenty-two-year-old mail clerk, Richard, who was currently showing Mr. Miller just how much he appreciated him via fellatio.

As I clicked away with my camera I felt a growing weird feeling in the pit of my stomach. I'd taken pictures of others doing more explicit acts than this but for some reason watching young Richard take Mr.

Miller in his mouth like it was the best thing in the world made my stomach flip.

I shook off the feeling and took a few more pictures before looking at my phone. Still nothing.

I hadn't heard a peep from Walter or my profile since I had gone into the Guy 4 U headquarters. It made me wonder if maybe I had come off wrong. Or maybe my picture wasn't quite right?

Once I had done the video interview, Walter had me fill out the rest of my profile online. Or really, Trisha filled it out. I had no idea finding a mate in the human world was so hard.

In heaven, if we wanted to have a child someone was assigned to us. Since I was a soldier procreating wasn't really something I had been interested in. The only person I would have even considered having a child with was gone.

A pinch of sadness hit me but I brushed it off.

Sighing, I took a few more photos making sure I got Mr. Miller's face in each shot before I began to pack up. Just as I started to climb down the fire escape my phone beeped.

Dropping onto the next platform I glanced at the screen. A smile spread across my face when I saw Adara's name flash across the screen.

Pressing the button on the screen to answer it, I said, "How is it you know just when I need you to call?"

"It's a gift," I could practically hear the smirk in her voice. Adara wouldn't know humble if it bit her in her thousand dollar pants. "Why? Were you thinking of jumping off a building? Testing that theory we talked about before?"

I chuckled, "We were drunk off our butts when we talked about that and no, I don't have any flights of fancy right now. Just some pictures to deliver and demons that need to call me already."

"Is that why you are showing up in the middle of the air next to an art gallery?" she paused and then in a teasing voice asked, "Are you still taking dirty porno pictures for money? Oh, how the mighty have fallen." I'd have bitten her head off at mentioning anything to do with falling, but I knew she didn't mean anything by it.

"They aren't porno pictures. They are evidence in an infidelity case," I held the

105

phone between my shoulder and ear as I climbed down the next ladder.

"If you say so. You have your fetishes and I have mine."

I didn't bother to correct her. Adara's fetishes came at the price of playing with the enemy. I didn't exactly approve of her actions but she'd saved my life and I didn't trust anyone more. What she did in her personal time was her business.

"So about these demons," Adara started, "Do you need back up?"

"Nah, I've got it."

"Are you sure? You know all you have to do is ask," she said a bit overeager to be included.

"And make you come out of retirement? No way," I scoffed, "It's just a silly case."

"Well, tell me about it."

"Uh, I really shouldn't. It's police business," I argued. It was bad enough I let Trisha in on what I do for the police. Telling Adara would be pushing it.

"Well? Is it dangerous?"

I snorted, "When is it not?" I shook my head though she couldn't see it, "Let's just say this case is making me do things I never thought I would ever do."

"Worse than the time you had to pretend to be a hooker to catch that one client cheating? Remember the fishnets?" she laughed a full-chested laugh that made me giggle.

"Yep, even worse than that."

"Ooh," she drew the word out, "Now you have to tell me!"

"I can't. It's classified," I paused on the last platform and leaned against the railing.

"Just tell me some of it. You don't have to tell me the specifics," Adara urged me.

"I have to go on a date." I waited for what I was sure was going to be laughter at my expense but it never came.

"Well, that's good."

I frowned at the seriousness in her voice, "No, it's not. You should see the get-up Trisha had me buy for this crap. Dresses and heels. Tiny purses that have no use but to look nice."

Adara giggled. Then kept giggling for a good few minutes. I crossed my free arm over my chest and tapped my foot, "Are you done?"

"Sorry," she cleared her throat, "You have to admit it is quite funny. You are acting like this is the worst thing in the world to happen to you, but you want to know what I think?"

"Does it matter?"

She ignored my question and kept talking, "I think you need to get out there. You might have been able to fool the humans around you but you are still closed off to those around you. Maybe this will help you come out of your shell."

"I don't need to get out of my shell. I'm fine."

"Oh really? How many friends do you have?" I opened my mouth to answer but she kept going, "not counting me or those employed by you, or who are employing you."

She had me there. Besides her and Trisha, the only other person I considered a friend would be Sid but some days I wasn't even sure about that.

"I don't need any more friends. I'm not staying," I reminded her, "as soon as I get my wings back, I'm out of here."

"I know that, but Muriel," she said softly, "What if you never find them or the demons that did it to you? Isn't it better to build a life here than live an empty existence only focused on revenge?"

My jaw clenched at her words, "I will find them. I have to."

"But what if you don't?"

"I will worry about it then," I snapped as I shoved off the railing making the metal clang.

"What are you doing?" she asked at the noise.

"Climbing down a fire escape," I descended the last ladder and landed on the ground next to the street. I turned around to head toward the meeting spot I'd told Trisha to meet me at in a few minutes, but stopped short at the people blocking my way.

"Ma'am, we'll need you to come with us," a police officer said, his hands on his hips. Next to him stood a red-faced Richard and a pissed off Mr. Miller.

Crap.

"Adara I'll have to call you back."

* * *

I TAPPED MY FINGERS in a rapid beat against the metal of the interview table and sighed, "I've already told you. I'm a Private Investigator hired by Mr. Miller's wife."

The detective, who had introduced himself as my worst nightmare, Aikens, leaned across the table and sneered, "Then where is your license?"

"I didn't bring it with me."

Aikens shoved off the table, "A likely story."

I had a feeling he was being sarcastic but knew better than to ask him about it.

"Look, call Sergeant Thompson. He'll vouch for me," I gestured out the interview door. I'd been taken to the East Side precinct, a place I'd never had the pleasure of visiting and if this was the way they treated their suspects I didn't plan to visit them again.

"The sergeant doesn't need to be bothered with the likes of you. He has a murder case to solve," I could hear a bit of bitterness in his voice as he said it. Ah, there was some discontent in the ranks of the LAPD.

"Fine. I get a phone call, don't I?" Aikens reluctantly nodded, "Then I'd like to call my assistant."

"What for?"

"To prove to you I'm not lying, of course," I forced myself not to roll my eyes at him. Really? Why else would I need to call them?

In all honesty, if I really wanted to leave I could. They wouldn't be able to stop me. Maybe if enough bullets riddled my body they could, but physically? It would take at least ten of them to match my strength. Opening objects on earth were quite a challenge when I first got here. I broke more than my fair share of doors and jars.

"Alright, you can call your assistant, but I'm going to be right here to make sure you don't try any funny business," the detective plopped down in the seat opposite of me and slid his phone across the table for me.

Picking it up, I dialed the number for the office, praying that Trisha had gone back when I didn't show up at our meeting spot. After the first ring, Trisha's panicked voice came on the line. "Mary? Is that you?"

"Yeah, it's me," I sighed.

"Where are you? I waited at the spot and then you never showed up. I thought maybe those demons had gotten a hold of you or something."

My eyes glanced over to the officer before I answered, "No, I'm fine. I did get arrested though."

"Arrested!" I pulled the phone away from my ear as Trisha's voice hit sonic level. "What for?"

I turned to the detective, "What was I arrested for again?"

He leaned forward on his elbows and smiled as he said, "Trespassing and invasion of privacy."

"Did you get that, Trish?" I said into the phone, my eyes still on the detective. Aikens was attractive enough if it hadn't been for the permanent snarl on his face. Though, I'd come to learn that all cops tend to look the same to me after a while. The same straight-faced expression, eyes that could easily go dark at a moment's notice. I'd pity their job if I hadn't been in their shoes before. Aikens wasn't much different.

"Yeah. Do you need me to call Thompson?" she asked and then there was movement in the background like she was getting up from her desk.

"And bring my license please."

"Be there in twenty."

"Thanks." I hung up the phone and handed it back to Aikens. "She'll be here soon."

Aikens snatched the phone back and tucked it into his pocket. He then leaned back in his seat, his hands crossed over his stomach as he studied me.

I sat in my chair, my gaze meeting his. He was trying to make me nervous enough to give away something. It wouldn't work. I was telling the truth and there was nothing else I could give.

"You're not from around here, are you?" Aikens finally asked after at least ten minutes.

"No. Not really."

"How long have you been a dick, Mary?" he exaggerated the word making it sound dirtier than what he meant.

I shrugged, "A few years now."

His lips quirked up at the edges, "I bet you just love taking dirty pictures. They just rile you up, a girl like you," Aikens' eyes trailed up and down my form, what he could see of it anyways.

"What's that supposed to mean?" my eyebrows rose. I wasn't sure I liked where this conversation was going.

"You know what I mean," he argued, his gaze focusing on my lower section, "You like to play hardball, be one of the guys. Tell me, Mary. Do you like to eat pussy as well?"

"Wouldn't know," I answered honestly. I wasn't offended per se. It was a reasonable question in my mind. But I knew that he was trying to bait me by asking what others would find inappropriate questions.

My response caught him off guard, his brows rose and his eyes jerked up to mine, "You're a hard one to crack, aren't you Mary?"

"That's what they say."

"Alright, that's enough of that," Sergeant Thompson said as he opened the door.

I jumped to my feet, ecstatic to see a friendly face, "Hey, Thompson."

"Wiles," he nodded to me and then leveled his eyes on Aikens, "What do I hear about you giving my specialist a hard time?"

"Specialist?" Aikens looked me over disbelief on his face. "You didn't tell me you were a specialist. What do you specialize in?"

"The occult," I said plainly, making his face scrunch up even more.

"Well, now that we all know," Thompson stepped in before Aikens could say anything else, "I need my specialist for that murder case we are working on. I can't be having her locked up for stupid shit like . . ." he paused looking to me and Aikens.

"Trespassing and invasion of privacy," Aikens growled, "She will still need to be processed. We can't just give her over."

"What for?" Thompson asked, "For taking a few photos of someone who was stupid enough to do it with the window open? You ask me . . . he wanted to get caught."

"But Sergeant, you can't just—" Aikens started, but Thompson cut him off.

"I can't what detective?" Thompson dared him to answer the question.

115

Aikens was smarter than he looked and swallowed down his words, though his jaw clenched tight, "Nothing. You can do whatever you want."

"That's what I thought. Come on, Wiles," Thompson waved me through the interview room door, "I hear you've got a date."

"I do?" I followed him out, leaving a fuming detective behind.

9

THE DATE WAS CLEARLY not the guy we were looking for.

First off, his profile didn't even remotely give off that he was looking for young innocent women to sacrifice. I mean come on, his description said he was looking for a good time. Not something you would say to someone who supposedly wanted to connect with other virgins.

Secondly, when he had messaged me— or Marcella as my profile says—he'd called me sexy and wanted to know if I wanted to hang out, or whatever. He was definitely something, but not our guy.

Thirdly, his name was Dean. That kind of name just screamed only looking for a good time. If this was our guy, I'd eat my foot.

117

"I'm not going out with him," I shook my head at Trisha, waving my hands in front of me as if to ward him off, "No way."

"Why not? He looks . . . cute," Trisha made a face at the barely visible head shot. Either he had been moving while the picture was being taken, or he was just really bad at taking photos. I couldn't make out more than he had brown hair and a semi-large nose.

"I don't care. We know it's not the guy, so going out with him would be a waste of time," I argued back.

"I think you should do it."

"You do?" my gaze shot over to Thompson who was sitting on the couch.

"Yes, it will help keep up appearances. If you only wait around for the one we're looking for, then they're going to suspect something," he leaned forward and opened his hands to me, "Look, I know it's not ideal but we can't lose this chance. This is the only lead we have. Take one for the team, Wiles."

"Easy for you to say, you don't have to sit through . . ." I looked over Trisha's shoulder to read where he had suggested we go, ". . . 'a night of partying and getting

118

to know each other intimately',", my nose scrunched up at the italics around the last word. Clearly, he was expecting more than a date.

"Sounds like he's a blast," Trisha looked up at me with fake enthusiasm.

I glared down at her.

"If not him, then it will be someone else even worse," Thompson offered me a weak smile, "Might as well break the ice with low expectations."

"Think of it as practice for the real thing," Trisha tried to convince me, but I wasn't biting. There was no way this was practice.

For the real thing I would be putting my best face forward and try to get as much information out of my date as possible. There would be blood, carnage, and hopefully a whole lot of exorcised demons. Nothing intimate about it.

* * *

IN THE END, THOMPSON and Trisha convinced me. "More like tricked me," I muttered under my breath as I stood in the long line outside a club called Mystic.

Dean had been over the moon when I had agreed to go out with him. Apparently, that didn't translate into being on time for our date. I'd been waiting in the line for about twenty minutes and still no sight of my mysterious date.

I moved forward in the line once more, the three-inch heels Trisha had manipulated me into wearing, clicking on the concrete. I leaned out of the line to check how much further until I was inside.

Forever.

The line was massive and the likelihood that I'd get inside before midnight was looking slim. I sighed and pulled my phone out of my tiny purse.

The dress I was wearing this time hit mid-thigh and had an open back and a modest front. The black material clung to me like a second skin. When I'd asked Trisha how this outfit would help with the case, she'd just shrugged, "It won't, but every girl deserves a little black dress. This is your chance to try yours out."

"Hey sexy," a voice shouted before a hand grabbed a handful of my backside. I grabbed the hand and gave it a twist as I spun around on my heel.

"Woah! What's the big idea?" the guy who vaguely looked like the image of Dean online winced as I held his wrist in a tight grip.

"Dean?" I asked, not yet letting go of him.

"Yeah, that's me," I let him go and watched as he rubbed his wrist. "Man, I didn't know you were into kinky shit like that. If I had known, I'd have taken you to a much different club."

I rolled my eyes and crossed my arms over my chest, "You're late."

Dean scratched the back of his head—a head that barely reached my chin. "Yeah, sorry about that. My ma needed me to do a few chores before I went out, but I'm here now and you look great," his eyes undressed me as he licked his lips.

I take back all I said about demons being lechers. This guy was worse.

121

"Thanks," I grumbled before gesturing toward the line, "we'll probably be here a while. Might as well get to know each other."

"What?" he leaned out and glanced at the length of the line before turning back to me, "Nah, don't worry about it. Here, follow me."

Before I could object he took my hand and started leading us up the line, causing all kinds of unrest among those waiting. Once we got to the front, a large man, muscles almost bursting from his shirt, blocked our path.

"Hey, Leo," Dean smiled and high-fived the man, "me and my lady friend here are on the list," he slid his arm around my waist and pulled me tight against him with a satisfied grin. I forced a smile at Dean.

Leo, as Dean had called him, didn't even look at the list, but gestured for us to go inside. Dean wasted no time and ushered me into the loud building, the people in the line behind us still shouting in protest.

The music of the club pulsating through my veins. The beat thundered in my ears making it impossible to even think. People must not come to the club to be aware of their surroundings because the lighting wasn't any better.

Dimly-lit alcoves and strobe lights shooting across the dance floor were the only forms of lighting. The club members moved through the crowd as if of one mind.

The hand on my waist tightened and I looked down to my date. Dean's mouth moved but I couldn't hear him over the music. "What?" I shouted in hopes to get him to repeat himself.

"I said," he said back, a bit louder this time, "do you want to get a drink?"

Instead of trying to yell over the music, I nodded and let him lead me through the throng of people.

The amount of body heat made my skin perspire and the room almost uncomfortably warm. When Dean handed me a drink, I didn't even bother to ask what it was but took a big swig.

The alcohol burned as it went down my throat and I felt the effect immediately. My head felt light and the unease at being there melted away.

"Alright! Let's dance?" Dean downed his drink, and before I knew it I was out on the dance floor with the rest of L.A.'s crazies.

Dancing was not new to me. I had danced before in my existence, but nothing like what I was doing now. The music had an almost violent tune to it, making those who danced to its beat throw their bodies around the dance floor.

The slow sensual dance I'd seen at The Night Owl was nothing like the grinding couples at Mystic. Dean tried to copy the others but his movements were jerky and stiff. Instead of trying to match his dance, I found my own rhythm.

My hands moved up along my sides and swept into my hair. I held them above my head as I whipped my hips from side to side. Closing my eyes, I let the music fill me.

Suddenly, I felt lightheaded. I opened my eyes and the world swam. Before I could collapse to the ground, Dean's arm were around me, ushering me off the dance floor and into one of the darkened alcoves.

"A bit of a lightweight, aren't you?" Dean chuckled, helping me into the lounge chair. He sat down next to me, a bit closer than I would normally be comfortable with, but my head was swimming too much for me to comment on it.

"I don't know what's wrong with me," I murmured. Usually, alcohol had the same kind of effect on me as caffeine. I felt it ten times as hard as a human and it usually left my system just as fast as it hit it. This though was different.

"It's alright. You're just having fun," Dean's voice reassured me, One of his arms was wrapped around the back of the couch keeping me close to him as his other hand slid up my inner thigh.

"Stop," I tried to push his hand away but my limbs were like wet noodles.

"Come on sexy, you loved it out there on the dance floor," Dean leaned his weight into me, pushing me down onto the couch. I glanced out to see if anyone would come to my rescue but it was so dark in the club and the music so loud no one was paying us any mind.

I tried to get my legs to work, but they were as useless as my hands. Dean's hands, on the other hand, were busy reaching under my dress. His fingers grabbed at the material of my underwear and jerked them to the side. Cool digits prodded at me and then Dean was maneuvering himself between my thighs.

The drink he had given me must have had something in it. Anger filled me at how stupid I had been for just taking a drink from someone I had just met.

I knew what he was planning on doing. I might be a virgin, but I wasn't an idiot. I knew from the beginning this had been a bad idea but no, everyone had told me I should get out more so I listened. Trisha was so going to hear about this later.

But first. Like with all substances the effects of the drug he had put in my drink began to wear off. The cloudiness in my mind cleared and my hands and arms began to work again.

Dean was completely oblivious to what was happening. His mind too focused on trying to get his pants unzipped and keep me in place at the same time.

"Oh, Dean?" I called out reaching my hands up to cup his face.

He glanced up at me in confusion only for his expression to turn to one of pain as I slammed my forehead into his face. Jerking back from me, he gave me enough room to get out from under him. I stood to my feet, adjusting my dress as I went.

Dean scrambled out of the booth, his nose bleeding and his pants around his ankles. "What? How?" he sputtered at me. "I gave you enough to knock a horse out. How are you still walking?"

A chilling smile crept up my face as I stepped toward him. Each step Dean stumbled back, trying to pull his pants up before someone saw. I shot forward grabbing him by the scruff of his collar and shoved him against the wall.

"You think drugging people is fun, do you?" I snarled.

"What? I don't know what you are talking about," he gave a nervous chuckle.

"Don't try to play dumb with me. You just admitted you had put something in my drink," my hand latched onto his arm and gave it a slight squeeze, making Dean's eyes bug out in pain.

"Stop. Stop already," he gasped, "I admit it. I tried to drug you. I'm sorry. I won't do it again."

I let the veil that covered his soul drop down. I didn't know why I hadn't done this before when we first met. Maybe then I would have been more on my toes. The inky color of his soul was a blaring warning sign to stay far away from this guy.

"Do you know what they do with guys like you in hell?" I hissed in his ear. Now that the veil was down, my angelic power rippled along my skin and by the chill that ran through Dean I knew he could feel it.

"No," his Adam's apple bobbed frantically up and down.

"Well, neither do I," I squeezed his arm tighter until he let out a whimper, "but I do know that what they did to me will be nothing compared to what they will do to scum like you."

Letting go of him, I let him fall to the ground with a thump. No one even stopped what they were doing during the whole interaction. It didn't surprise me. Humans were frivolous creatures. More interested in getting their latest fix than helping someone in need.

Sex. Alcohol. Drugs. Even attention. All of them were an addiction that they couldn't kick, and most didn't want to—or didn't even know they were falling, but I did.

I always knew.

10

WHEN I HAD TOLD Trisha what had happened she had been beside herself with guilt.

"It's my fault," she'd cried out, "I pressured you into going and look what happened. You almost got date-raped."

"It's fine, Trisha. Really," I had patted her on the shoulder, "he didn't get very far. The drug wasn't that strong."

I had altered the story a bit. I couldn't very well tell her that the drug had worn off because I was a supernatural being and human substances didn't work too well on me. She'd have had a fit.

If she ever found out about what I was, I knew I'd be in for it. I wouldn't hear the end of her questions. I could just imagine how much worse it will be with that knowledge in her head. It was bad enough when she'd found out I exorcised demons.

After her meltdown, it was safe to say I hadn't gone on any other dates. Then thankfully, a few days later I finally had a request from another guy to meet him at The Night Owl Bar and Grill.

"Are you sure this dress is alright?" I twisted around trying to look myself over. For this date, Trisha had dressed me in a tighter dress that was pale plume in color. It clung to my figure and made it close to impossible to move in, let alone put my gun anywhere.

"It's fine. You look hot," she gushed next to me as we walked into the Night Owl.

"I still think I should have brought my gun. I could have put it in my purse or something," I grumbled shifting the thin strap of the bag she had insisted I wear. At least, my shoes were walkable.

Trisha snorted, "No woman in the history of time has ever been able to find anything in her purse in less than five minutes. You'd be dead before you found it. Besides," she lowered her voice as we came closer to the bar, "these are demons;

your gun won't help you much anyway remember?"

My lips turned down. Just because it wouldn't help didn't mean it wasn't nice to have. If I ended up surrounded it would be an easy way to get myself out of there, but I could see her point.

"You're not allowed in here," a deep voice said from behind the bar.

"How does he do that?" Trisha leaned over and cast her eyes on the muscular back of Sid who hadn't turned to greet us as he counted the cash in the register.

I didn't answer her as I sidled up to the end of the bar, "She's not staying."

"Yeah," Trisha added, "so don't get your panties in a wade. I'm just seeing my bestie off on her first date."

"It's not my first date," I objected but she waved me off.

"The other one doesn't count."

"Date?" this made him turn around. The moment his eyes swept over me I felt a heat cover my skin and then settle low in my stomach. What was it with this place? "You clean up well, angel."

I scowled at his compliment, "It's just a dress."

132

"A very form-fitting dress," he didn't even try to pretend not to be leering at me, "If you'd come in here like that more often, I'd have to beat the customers back."

Trisha laughed, but when I glared at her she covered it up with a cough, "Sorry. I have this thing. Well, anyways," she moved back from the counter, "I'm going to get going. Underage and all. You," she pointed at me, "call me. And you," Trisha turned her attention to Sid who gave her a lopsided grin, "keep your hands to yourself, pretty boy."

"Hey, I'll keep my hands wherever she wants them to be," he leaned onto the surface of the bar, giving me a wink.

Rolling my eyes, I waved to Trisha before turning back to Sid, "You seem better."

"What do you mean?"

"Last time you didn't seem like you were in a very good mood."

"Oh."

Oh. That was it. That's all I got. He's borderline rude to me, then all smiles today, and all I get is 'oh'.

Men.

"So, you have a date?" he changed the subject, "And it's your first? Do you not go on dates in heaven?"

"No."

"Not even little ones?" he squeezed his fingers together until there was barely any air between them.

"I had other things on my mind."

"Like what? Playing your harp? Lying on a cloud?"

I snorted, "I couldn't play a harp if I tried. And who lies on clouds?"

Sid shrugged, "I'm not an angel, I don't know what it's like up there."

"And I'm not going to tell you."

"Ah, why not? Throw a guy a bone. It's not every day someone has bonified proof that heaven exists," he smirked at me.

My eyes shot to the guy just two seats down from us whose attention just got piqued.

"He's kidding," I quickly said to him. Luckily he simply sniffed and went back to his drink.

"You," I hissed, pushing at Sid's shoulder, "need to watch what you say."

"Fine. Just tell me this," he leaned closer to me until he was only a few inches from my face, "How's the sex in heaven?"

"Ugh," I shoved him away from me, "You are worse than a demon, I swear."

"Come on," he held his hands up defensively, "you can't blame a guy for being curious. If you've had mind-blowing celestial orgasms, I need to up my game."

I scoffed at his words, "Even if I had mind-blowing celestial orgasms as you say, what makes you think that I would ever be comparing them to you?"

He pressed his hands against the edge of the counter in almost a push-up position, "Because everyone eventually gives in to me. They always do."

"Well, I feel sorry for them."

"Oh, yeah?"

"Yeah."

"Well, I feel sorry for whoever is your date tonight. Because the only person getting into those pristine panties of yours is God himself," he waved a hand in the general direction of my lower half.

"For your information, my *date* won't be getting anywhere near there. This is a job, *not a real date.*"

"Speaking of jobs. What did I tell you about doing that job in my bar? A customer found your little friend in the bathroom clean knocked out."

I shrugged, "At least he wasn't dead."

Sid gave a short laugh. "I'd have rather he'd been. A dead body I could have taken care of, but a lawsuit I can't."

"Is he suing you?"

"No, but he could have. That's why I don't want you doing it here, not to mention it would drive all my customers away," he swept a hand across the bar area.

"Fine. No more demon-extermination on your property. Got it."

"Good," Sid nodded. He looked toward the door and then back to me, "So when is your date coming anyways? It's bad form to be late on a first date."

"Any minute now and it's a fake date, so I don't care if they are late," I wouldn't care if they were an hour late and wearing a burlap sack, as long as they showed me where they were taking the women.

"Then, maybe I should show you what a real date would be like? After your fake date and all," his eyes darkened and he watched me intently.

I was hard pressed to take him up on his offer just simply for curiosity's sake. What I'd told him was true. I hadn't dated in heaven. I hadn't ever had intercourse, or sex as humans seemed to more frequently call it. There were so many humans on earth ruining theirs and other's lives to get it that I wanted to know what all the fuss was about.

And God help me, but I felt like a night with Sid would be a night to remember.

Before I could accept his offer though, the door to the bar opened causing Sid to stiffen. He didn't look to see who had entered but simply picked up a glass and started cleaning it.

I slowly turned in my seat until I was facing the person who had walked in. I didn't need to ask to know it was my date. I'd seen his picture.

Dark hair, tousled and styled like what was popular in Trisha's magazines. Pale blue eyes and a strong jaw. He was nothing like sleazy Martin. He was all muscle, and had half a head on me.

Not letting his size intimidate me, I slid off the bar-stool and approached him. I put on my best smile and held a hand out to him, "Owen? I'm Mary."

Owen's gaze made a slow path from my face and down my body, leaving a sick feeling in my stomach before he reached out and clasped my hand. Giving it a bit of squeeze that would have made a lesser angel wince, he smirked, "You're prettier than I would have thought."

I frowned. If he had watched my video, or even looked at my profile, he'd have known what I looked like. I was beginning to wonder if I was dealing with a lower-level demon this time at all.

"Uh, thanks. Should we grab a table?" I offered, thumbing back toward one of the booths near the back.

"Sure, babe. Whatever you want," he wrapped his arm around my lower waist, his hand landing on the swell of my butt.

I bit my inner cheek to keep myself from drop kicking the guy. As we walked by the bar, Sid glanced up at me and was trying to tell me something with his eyes but I couldn't understand what it was.

I let Owen lead me to the booth nearest the back door, like all the other victims, my unease crawling up my throat.

To ease some of the tension, I cleared my throat and said, "So Owen, tell me about yourself. What do you do?"

"Hopefully, you later," his lips quirked up at the comment, as if I was supposed to think it was charming.

I forced a smile, "Well, let's just see how this goes first before we hit the bedroom?"

"Whatever you say, babe," he grabbed my hands in his, his fingers stroking provocatively along my arms. Each touch made my skin crawl, and the urge to pull my hands back ate at me.

What the hell was with this guy? I let the veil that kept me sane drop, and stared at Owen. My date. And a very dark and powerful demon.

His power startled me so much that I jerked my hands back without meaning too. Owen's brows shot up, but I brushed it off by adjusting my purse next to me.

Owen wasn't just possessed by *a* demon but at least an upper-level demon. Meaning I was in big trouble.

I'd told Trisha I would need my damn gun.

When Sid approached our table, I almost got up and kissed him right there.

"Sid, hey," I said with more enthusiasm than I had from talking to him before.

"Did you guys want to order?"

"Yes!" I practically jumped in my seat. "You're hungry, aren't you?" I glanced to Owen briefly before turning back to Sid without waiting for an answer. "I'll have the special with extra ketchup and a glass of—"

"We aren't staying."

"We aren't?" I questioned Owen.

"No, we have a reservation somewhere else," he stood from the table, not so subtly shoving Sid aside, "Somewhere better."

"But I like this place," I argued reluctantly letting him pull me to my feet.

Widening my eyes at Sid, trying to signal for him to save me but apparently, my eye messages didn't come through any better than his had because he just crossed his arms over his chest and stood aside.

"Come on, babe," he wrapped his arm around my waist, pulling my tight against his side, "Let's go out this way, I parked around back."

"Uh, okay," I stumbled a bit at the fast pace Owen had set, making him have to practically carry me to the door.

The back door smacked open and Owen shoved me through making me fall to the concrete, scraping my knees. *Ouch.*

"What the hell, Owen?" I brushed myself off and tried to get to my feet without my dress going further up my thighs.

That was when the laughing started. Not just one person's laughter but several. My gaze moved slowly from the ground to the sound around me.

Owen stood by the now-closed door and a demon-drenched flunky on either side. They looked down at me like I was an all-you-can-eat buffet. It didn't give me the same kind of warm and fuzzy feeling I usually got. Instead it made me want to wish I had never said yes to this job.

In the words of Trisha, Fuckity, fuck, fuck, fuck.

11

WHY ARE ALL DEALS done in alleyways? Why couldn't they be in a brightly-lit area with lots of people? I supposed it was too much to ask for.

I was outnumbered and pretty much screwed. I had no weapon and my talisman was in my tiny purse that was lying five feet away from me. The likelihood of me getting to it before they figured out what I was doing was pretty slim.

It didn't keep me from trying, though.

Trying not to draw attention to what I was going for, I scrambled to my feet and put my back to the purse with my hands up. "Look, guys, I don't know what kind of kinky stuff you're into but I'm a one-man kind of woman."

The demon-possessed men laughed at my comment and jostled each other. Owen took a step forward, his large beefy hands reaching for me, "You'll be singing a different tune pretty soon."

"I don't think so," I gave a nervous laugh and kept inching my feet backward until the heel of my shoe made the metal hooks of the bag clink.

Before Owen's hand could grab me, I ducked down and grabbed the bag. Clutching it to my chest, I fumbled to get it open while they demons laughed at me. Trisha was right; no woman could ever find anything in her purse in less than five minutes. Hell, I couldn't even get the thing open in that amount of time.

"No one is going to help you, sweetheart," Owen snarled trying to rip the bag from my hands. "No use trying to call for help."

"I don't want to call anyone," I argued through clenched teeth as I yanked back on the bag. "I just need my..."

Just then the bag tore open, scattering the whole two items in the bag onto the ground. The first being my cell phone, which shattered when it hit the concrete, making me wince. Phones weren't cheap, but unfortunately, in this world it was a necessary evil. I didn't know how I was going to get a new one now.

Priorities, Mary. I shook my head, giving my phone one last sad look before searching out the second, more important item.

My talisman.

"What's this?" one of the demons who had taken up house in a guy with a nasty scar down the left side of his face, held up my talisman by the beaded chain.

"Give that to me, my father gave that to me. It's the only thing I have left of him," I'd used the story often when getting searched. You'd be surprised how often people don't want you to take jewelry, even inexpensive jewelry into their workplace.

Scarface glanced at Owen still holding the charm. "What do you say, boss?"

Boss? Did my exorcism of Martin really call for bringing the big guns in? It didn't bode well for the rest of the night.

"Give the girl her necklace," Owen smiled eying me up and down, "Let her cling to what little she has left in this world."

His words made his fellow demons laugh, and then Scarface, thankfully tossed the talisman toward me. My eyes stayed on the charm. I reached out and grabbed it, and in my distraction Owen grabbed me.

Letting out a squeal, I tried to pull away from his grasp, but he didn't budge. Humans were easy to get away from, but Owen must be a far higher-level demon than I had realized, because I actually had to work for it.

"You're strong for a human," Owen commented, before throwing me over his shoulder, "this should be fun."

Hanging over his shoulder, my stomach rolled. Owen might be able to hide what he was on the outside, but this close to him there was no doubt what he was inside of his body. Like bugs beneath my skin, his dark energy licked at my flesh. If I wasn't trying to keep what I was under wraps, I'd have tried to exorcise his butt right then.

"Let's go, boys, we're wasting the moon." I swung from side to side as he turned to look at his companions. Then Owen was moving and I bounced against his back. Clutching my talisman in my hand until it bit into my skin, I ground my teeth. I hoped they weren't going far.

145

"Hey, boss," the other demon asked, "ain't she a bit quiet?"

"What do you mean?"

"I mean, the others were kicking and screaming so much we had to knock them out. This one hasn't given us that much trouble."

Crap. I forgot I was supposed to act like a normal human woman would and fight to get away. Since I wanted to be taken I hadn't thought about trying to fight too much. I figured once they got me I could just pretend to give up.

Owen stopped in his tracks and turned slightly, there was a thud and then a grunt from the demon. "Don't ask questions. This one is smarter than the others, is all. I knew it from the beginning," he continued walking as he talked, "She knows it is pointless, don't you, Mary?" Owen patted me on the butt and I fought the urge to make a face.

I stayed silent at his question until he smacked me harder on the butt, making it sting, "I asked you a question."

Gritting my teeth, I snapped, "It's pointless."

"Now, let's load her in the car," a beep signaled that someone had unlocked a vehicle sounded.

I snorted, but quickly held back my laugh. I was being kidnapped, about to be sacrificed, and I was laughing over the fact that the demons were worried about having their car stolen.

God help me.

Next thing I knew, I was being shoved into the backseat of a black SUV with Owen in the front passenger seat and the demon who had been pretty quiet until this point in the driver seat. Scarface got into the back as well, leering at me. I moved as far away from him as I could which only made him laugh.

"What, you don't want to be by old Willy?" he chuckled and wagged his eyebrows at me as the car began to move.

Keeping my eyes on the passing street signs to keep in mind later, I retorted, "Not particularly."

While trying to remember where we were going was necessary, I was also trying not to react to his name. I didn't know if it was his demon name or the guy he inhabited, but either way, it was not instilling fear in anyone's heart.

"That's all right," he leered at me, "soon enough you'll want everything I, or anyone else, decide to give you."

"That's not likely," I snorted, shifting in my seat to fix my dress which had moved up after I'd been manhandled. "God himself wouldn't be able to get me to open my legs to you, Scarface."

"What'd you call me?"

Berating a demon was probably not a good idea. Especially since I was supposed to be playing the victim, but I was getting tired of being tossed around like a rag doll. I did not play the damsel in distress well.

"You heard me," I taunted, "how did you get that scar anyways?" I gestured to his face, "One too many women tell you no?"

"Why, you bitch!" Scarface launched himself at me; his hand grabbed my shoulders. "I'm going to show you who's telling who no."

His hands were rough as he shoved them between my thighs. He tried to get himself between my legs, but I kicked my feet at him, making him grunt.

"Willy, leave her alone," Owen growled from the front.

"But, boss, you heard her."

Owen's hand came out from the front and shoved at Willy's shoulder. "I don't give a fuck if she insulted your mother, keep your hands to yourself. She's no good to us if you ruin her now."

Scarface frowned and moved back to his seat, though I could tell he didn't want to. And being the person I was, I couldn't leave it alone.

"You heard your master, get back on your leash."

Why Mary? Why must you poke the beast? I asked myself after the words came out of my mouth.

"That's it!"

Willy threw himself at me once more, his hands groped my breasts and underneath my dress.

"Get off me!" I shoved at his chest. He wasn't quite as strong as Owen was, so I could probably have thrown his butt through the car window if I wanted to.

Actually . . .

My hand searched for the door-handle and I jerked on it, causing the door to fly

149

open. Scarface flew out the door and onto the quickly passing pavement. The sound of him grunting when he hit the ground faded quickly as we kept moving down the street.

Before I could contemplate jumping out of the car, Owen's hand latched onto the back of my neck. Throwing me across the backseat, he reached out and pulled the door closed.

"Now, why'd you have to go and do that?" he asked as if asking the time of the day, "Now, we have to go back for him, and he's not going to be very happy with you."

I glared at him.

"Boss," the demon driving the car said, "it's already nine o'clock if we go back for him, we'll be late."

"Fuck," Owen rubbed a hand over his face and then glared at me, "You cost me a man today. Now, I'm going to have to participate and believe me when I say you will pay for it."

Way to go, Mary.

The prospect of Owen joining the festivities did not bode well. Just from the outside, he was a bad motherfucker. When his full demon power was unleashed, I could imagine any human wouldn't last long.

Good thing I wasn't remotely human.

The car ride was quiet after Willy's departure. I could almost forget I was riding in a car full of demons and that I was on my way to get gang-raped to bring whoever they were trying to summon over.

As we left the city, it became all too real. "Where are we going?"

Owen glanced at me from over his shoulder. "Don't worry your pretty little head about that."

"If I'm going to die anyways, it wouldn't matter, now would it?" I reasoned.

He scoffed, "You are a piece of work, you know that?"

"So I've been told," I muttered.

"Fine. I'll indulge you," Owen turned in his seat so that he was able to face me, "We are going to a clearing where no one will be able to hear your screams of pain and . . ." his eyes skimmed over me as he licked his lips, "pleasure."

"The only pleasure I'll be having is when I'm stabbing you in your grinning face," I snarled.

He only laughed at my threat, "Oh, you will enjoy it, all right. You'll die with a smile on your face, and if you are lucky, you'll go to heaven and be with your father again," he nodded to the talisman wrapped around my wrist, "If you've been a naughty girl though . . ." he trailed off and then barked out laughing, "You might just get lucky enough to get a visit from me again."

The wince that filled my face was involuntary and caused Owen to grin in triumph. He had officially been able to crack my hard exterior.

Some women might have liked the promise of being touched by him. The body he inhabited was fairly attractive, but it was the creature inside that chilled my blood.

I knew inside that meat bag was a cruel and evil thing that wouldn't hesitate to rip me apart on a whim. The experience I'd had at the mercy of demons like him caused my scars to ache.

No.

I didn't want to be at his disposal, on earth or in hell.

My mind full of dark thoughts, I didn't even notice we had stopped until the passenger door opened and Owen offered me a hand.

"It's show time, girly. Time to put on your best face."

I ignored his hand with a frown and dropped from the car. The moment my feet hit the ground, I had the overwhelming urge to run.

I just knew something bad would happen tonight. While I had put myself in this situation on purpose, it wasn't going the way I'd hoped.

For starters, I didn't have my gun. It wouldn't help against the demons but it would make me feel better. Secondly, my phone was smashed. Any hope of the cops being able to track me was gone.

Thirdly, I'd counted on facing off a few low-level demons, not a high-power one like Owen. It made my decision to decline to have the cops follow me seem stupid now.

Lastly, if Owen was the boss of this little gathering, whoever they were summoning had to be ten times worse. I needed to know who that was so I could stop it. Meaning, I had to play the victim for a little bit longer.

Fortunately, one thing was going right. I had my talisman. So, I wasn't completely defenseless. Now, I only had to bide my time until they unraveled their plan to me. Then it was bye-bye demons, hello sweet vengeance.

Besides, I was an angel, what was the worst that could happen?

12

ONE POSITIVE I COULD look at was at least I wouldn't die under a crusty bridge.

My heels crunched on the gravel road and then turned silent as we walked across a field of grass. Owen hadn't been lying when he'd said they wanted to go somewhere no one would hear me scream. There wasn't anything for miles. Not even any streetlights.

I slowly made my way across the area, Owen at my back giving me a nudge every once in a while if I was going too slowly. Scarface hadn't showed up, thankfully, meaning one less demon to worry about.

The problem was I didn't know how many more were waiting for me up ahead. I could make out torches set up along the area as we approached. Then the chanting began.

"It's almost time," Owen said, eagerness in his voice, "Are you ready for this, Mary?"

I gave him a flat look. Really? He was going to ask me if I was ready to get tortured? I guess even the upper-level demons are stupid sometimes.

Owen laughed. "Don't worry, you will be. Once the boss gets here."

"Boss?" I asked confusion on my face, "But I thought you were the boss?"

The other demon stepped in and clapped Owen on the shoulder with a laugh. "This guy? He's just a lacky like the rest of us. The big man will be here soon and then the real fun begins."

"Shut up you," Owen growled shoving the demon away from him and then turned his gaze to me, "It would do for you to keep that mouth of yours closed or it will be worse for you."

"You mean worse than being raped and killed by a bunch of beef heads?"

His hand whipped up, whacking me on the side of the face. The shock of it knocked me to the ground.

My face stung from where he hit me, and I rubbed at it as I glared up at him. Now that hurt.

"You've got a smart mouth on you, and it's going to get you hurt," Owen reached down and didn't offer to help me up; instead he grabbed my arm and jerked me to my feet. Giving me a nasty smile, he almost dragged me toward the torches, "I can't wait."

While Owen might be in a hurry to get to business it seemed that the rest of his crew wasn't. They lounged around on metal chairs that had been set up near the iconic four poster bed in the middle of the area. The torches I had seen before went around the bed in a circle.

The symbols that had been at all the other crime scenes were missing. There was no blood, not even on the sheets that were surprisingly pristine white.

As if reading my mind, Owen said, "You should be lucky we even got a new bed and everything for this. You will be like a goddess being worshiped by her followers."

"Loved to death, huh?" I muttered, my eyes still on the bed.

"Now you are getting it," I glanced up at Owen long enough for him to smirk before he led me to the group of demons.

One. Two. Three. A total of five demons counting Owen, and the other demon whose name I still didn't know. Too bad Willy wasn't here for this.

"Hey, boss, where's Willy?"

Owen must have some kind of mind-reading powers, because I was just about to snark out a retort when he squeezed my arm tightly. "He had an emergency."

"An emergency?" a blond-haired man with a slight potbelly stood from one of the chairs. "What could be more important than this? We've been planning for months! And with the cops on our tail, we have to finish before—"

"I know!" Owen cut him off and then shoved me toward the little group, "Here. Get her tied up. I have to finish getting things ready before the boss gets here."

I fell into the waiting hands and they made my skin crawled. There was so much darkness in them. Their lust-filled gazes as they took in my clothes didn't help much either.

158

"She's a pretty one. Are you sure she's a virgin?" one of the other demons asked caressing a hand down my face.

Owen laughed at his question, "If you'd heard the mouth on that one you'd have no doubt she is one. There's a reason she was desperate enough to sign up for that site."

"Hey," I snapped, "I am not desperate." I struggled against the hands on me. They were low-level demons, so they weren't too hard to break free from.

Shoving to my feet, I stalked over to Owen. "Not every person who looks online for love is desperate." I pointed a finger at his chest. "You were online. Are *you* desperate?"

My comment made the other demons laugh, but Owen wasn't laughing. If anything, his power had grown as rage filled his face. This time his fist came at me, but I was ready for it.

I ducked out of the way and made for the torch line. Before I could get past the ring, multiple hands grabbed me. I kicked and bit at any flesh I could find. I wasn't playing the victim anymore. I was the victim.

"She's a feisty one all right," the potbelly demon laughed, his hand coming out to grab my breast, "I like them with some fight in them."

"Get her on the bed," Owen ordered, "we don't have time for this shit."

Pushing against the hands on me, I realized I had made a mistake. I had underestimated their power. They shouldn't have been able to catch me like that.

As they got me onto the bed, one demon holding each arm, and the potbellied man sitting on top, I realized how screwed I was.

No one would find me. I only had my talisman to defend myself, and as they tied my arms to the posts even that wasn't at my disposal. The need to find out whom they were summoning was gone, and now I just wanted to get out of here as fast as possible.

The ropes they'd used to tie my hands and legs to the posts were like the ones found on the previous victim. It was soft and didn't bite into my skin. The fact that they were seeking to ease my comfort was weirdly disturbing.

"What's the point of making sure I'm comfortable if you're just going to kill me?" I couldn't help but ask.

The demon with the potbelly let go of my arms now that they were secure and said, "The ropes aren't for you, precious," he trailed a fingertip down from my cheek, down my chin, and into the cleavage of my dress.

"Then who are they for?"

This time one of the demons who had tied my arm down answered, "The boss likes pretty things and compliant women."

"Well, he's going to be sorely disappointed then," I snapped, tugging on the ties around my hands. They were good and tight. Too bad I was surrounded by demons or I'd have broken them. They couldn't be that tough. I was supposed to be a weak, wimpy, human.

If only I was that lucky.

"Don't bother with trying to convince this one. She's a right bitch," an unfortunately familiar voice sounded.

A face I had hoped not to see again appeared in the dark. Scrapes and blood covered Willy's face and arms. His clothing was torn in places from where he had rolled across the road. The dark look in his eyes made me shiver involuntarily.

"Willy! You made it," the potbelly finally got off me and approached the scarred demon.

He clapped him on the back in greeting like they were old friends just hanging out for a barbeque. No sacrificing happening here folks, just a couple of pal's having a good time.

"What the hell happened to you man. Looks like you got into a fight with a cat."

Willy half-heartedly returned the greeting, his eyes firmly set on me, "Yeah, it was one tough pussy that was for sure, but I'm here now, and I'm more than ready to get this started."

The threat in his voice was clear and the glare in his eyes even more so. I forced myself to return his intense gaze with one of my own. I was not going to cower like a child to this vile creature.

"Thanks for waiting for me, boss." Willy's sarcasm was not lost on Owen and he gave him a nasty grin.

"If you'd listened to me then, you'd have been here on time. But it's too late now, I'm taking your place."

162

Willy's face colored. "No way. I want my chance at that bitch," he snarled, his eyes darting to where I lay.

Owen shook his head and pointed at Willy. "You had your chance, now I have a score to settle with her, and you will just have to suck it up. I outrank you."

"Not for long," Willy countered making Owen stomp over to him.

Shoving him in the chest, Owen asked, "Is that a challenge?"

Willy shoved him back and shouted, "You bet it is."

Plopping my head back down on the pillow, I sighed. Here I was, tied up to a bed, about to be sacrificed, or pretending to be, and they were arguing like children. How the underworld ever gets organized enough to function was beyond me.

"Hey, guys," the demon that had driven us here raised his hand and tried to interject, but they ignored him.

I watched the demon as he fought with himself. He seemed like the cowardly type. The kind that would joke around, but never really got involved. The fact that they weren't even paying him any mind showed how much respect he actually had in the group.

The demon tried once more to get their attention, but it was no use.

Letting out an aggravated groan, I pursed my lips and let out a high-pitched whistle.

That got their attention. Willy and Owen stopped fighting and all eyes were now on me. *Great, Mary, bring more attention to yourself.*

"Your boy is trying to say something," I nodded my head toward the demon that was trying to implode into himself at my mentioning him.

"What is it, Dawson?" Owen asked, his tone of voice showing he didn't really think he was worth Owen's time.

Dawson, as I now knew he was called, rubbed his hands together, glanced toward me and then back to Owen. "Well, you see . . ."

"Spit it out. We don't have much time left," Owen growled.

"See what I was going to say, boss . . . is that . . ." he licked his lips and looked back to me again. What was he waiting for? My approval? "Willy can have my spot."

"What?" Willy piped up. "No, Dawson. This is your first time. You won't get another chance to destroy something as delicious as this one."

I'd have been flattered had he not been talking about ripping me apart. Really, demons were so romantic.

Dawson shook his head. "No. I'm sure. You go for it. I'll wait until next time."

"There won't be a next time," Owen spoke up and clapped a hand on Dawson's shoulder, "this is your only chance to get in good with the boss. After this, he'll be on this plane. You never know when an opportunity like this will come back up."

"It's just . . ."

"What?" Owen asked, "what's got you backing out all of a sudden? She can't fight you, and when he gets here she won't even want to."

"Yeah," Willy agreed, the two now on the same side even though they had been about to tear each other apart a second before, "she'll be good and ready for you. You can't let this chance go to waste."

"But she's not right."

165

Willy and Owen exchanged a look and then their attention turned to me. I narrowed my eyes at them and gave them what Trisha called a one finger salute.

"Sure she's a bit more spirited than the others, but that's a good thing," Willy laughed and smacked Dawson on the back, making the other demon wince.

"No, I mean . . . she gives me a bad feeling. Like if we touch her . . ." he trailed off, his eyes going wide.

"What?" Owen asked.

Dawson shook his head and muttered, "We're all gonna die."

This made his whole group break out into laughter. If I hadn't been tied down, I'd have smacked the grins right off their faces. Dawson was one intuitive demon. I'd never met one that I felt sorry for, but I found myself wanting to get him away from these creatures.

I opened my mouth to tell them that he was right. They all were going to die tonight, and he didn't have to, but my words were caught in my throat as a ripple filled the air.

Suddenly, all thoughts were washed away, and everyone's attention zeroed in on a spot in the trees.

I didn't know how I knew someone was there, but it was like a feeling in my gut. I just knew. Then when he spoke that feeling changed.

"My fellow compatriots," a voice so smooth that it slid through me like a hand caressing my insides, "Thank you all for coming to this momentous occasion," a weird kind of tingle spread through me and settled between my thighs where a burning kind of need began.

The owner of the voice stepped out of the shadows and wore a face that even an angel would envy. The moment my eyes landed on him, combined with the unfamiliar feeling, caused a sense of dread to fill me.

When his dark chocolate colored eyes locked onto mine, I had to wonder, who exactly was playing whom?

13

THE BOSS. THE ONE in charge of this whole ordeal, stepped out from the shadows. He walked into the circle with his hands outstretched as if to embrace us.

Unlike the others he was dressed like a businessman. His blond hair was slicked back from his face, and his gaze stayed on me even as his minions approached him. It was like I was the only one that mattered.

"Boss," Owen said kneeling down before the man with the intense gaze. Owen ducked his head as if bowing to him before looking back up at him, "I'm sorry, we aren't quite ready yet. We still have to bless the sacrifice."

The man held up his hand and shushed him, "No matter. We shall do it now."

He moved across the grass like a prowling panther. His tongue darted out to lick his lips as he passed by his followers, each one coming to one knee as he came by. My eyes tracked him until he stopped beside the bed.

"Hello, pet," he purred, his eyes licking across my form.

My mouth became dry and I had to swallow several times to get any words out. "Hello," my voice came out breathless and weak. I hated it.

"We are going to have such a good time together," he reached out to cup my face, but stopped at Owen's voice.

"Boss, the moon."

The man that I most definitely didn't want to have touching me, pulled back. I let out a breath I didn't realize I had been holding and tugged on my bindings slightly. Now that his attention wasn't on me, I felt a bit more like myself.

I didn't know who this guy was, but I knew that I didn't want to have any sort of fun with him.

While I was trying to undo my restraints without using my angelic strength, Owen and the boss had stopped arguing and seemed to have come to some decision.

Owen came over to the bed and popped open a knife. My eyes darted to the blade and I licked my lips, "What are you going to do with that?"

Smirking at me, he said, "Not so smart-mouthed now that the boss is here, are ya? This," he twirled the knife in his hand, "is to get you ready. Can't have these pesky clothes getting in the way," he placed the knife on the top of my dress and cut into the material. Owen ripped it down the middle until it was more of a vest than anything.

The straps came next and then I was left in only my bra and underwear. Owen's fingers trailed along the inside of my thighs making me recoil. His eyes darted to my face, "You won't be cringing away from me soon. Soon you will be begging me to touch you."

I didn't answer him, instead, I said, "Aren't you going to take off my shoes?"

Confusion covered Owen's face and then Willy said, "Do as the lady asks. Besides, have you ever had high heels digging into your back? Not pleasant."

170

Owen turned from me and glared at Willy, "Then you take them off."

Returning Owen's glare, Willy stomped over to the bed and jerked my shoes off my feet. But before he could go back to his place, the big man boss from before said, "Mark her so we can start, William."

Willy nodded at him. "Of course, Asmodeus."

"Do not call me by name!" the demon spat, his eyes filling with rage, "Are we equals now? Are you a master demon?"

Asmodeus. The image that the Catholics had drawn of him didn't do him justice. Of course, he was housed inside a human, but still, he was one bad mama jama.

There were some demons you attacked head on, and there were others from whom you ran in the other direction and hoped they wouldn't follow. Asmodeus was one of the latter.

He wasn't called the demon of lust for nothing. Just being in the same area as him set my skin alight. A burning need settled between my thighs and my nipples hardened.

This feeling. This was what all the humans raved about. What they killed,

171

and ruined families over. Until now, I had thought I was immune to such feelings, but Asmodeus had proved me wrong.

Oh, so wrong.

Willy shook his head and stuttered, "No. No. I was out of line. I am sorry."

Asmodeus narrowed his eyes and gestured with a jerk of his hand, "Then get to work. I want to be in solid form before daybreak. This human form is so restricting," he adjusted his suit jacket with a grimace.

Willy nodded and then picked up a jar from the ground. Once he opened the top I could smell the sulfur as soon as it hit the air. He dipped his fingers into the jar and they came back a dark yellowish color.

As he approached me, I realized the jig was about to be up. They would know what I was any second now and I didn't have a plan.

The moment the powder touched my forehead the little holy power I had flared up. It lined my skin making the powder fall off of my face before it could ever stick.

Willy's face contorted in confusion before he tried to rub it on my forehead again. Still, it would not stick.

I couldn't help but laugh.

"What's the problem?" Asmodeus asked.

The demon above me turned from me to answer, "It won't stick, boss. No matter what I do."

"What? That's impossible. The human must be blessed with the sulfur from hell or they cannot be taken," Asmodeus explained through his rage, "Unless," his dark eyes turned to Owen, "you brought me an angel."

Those eyes then turned toward Willy and I. Willy's whole body shook as the air began to thicken. A slight tremor went through me at the pure evil pouring out of Asmodeus.

This was it. Time was up, and I wasn't waiting around to see how this temper tantrum would end.

"Oh, Willy," I cooed as I pressed the feather of the talisman into my hand. "I've been wanting to do this for a long time."

Willy's face contorted into confusion. Before he could ask me what I meant, I jerked on the rope wrapped around the wrist holding the talisman. His eyes widened and just as he was about to grab me I shoved the talisman against his forehead and forced my holy aura into him.

His mouth opened in a silent scream but he didn't fight back. It seemed that Willy was all talk and no bite.

The darkness inside him spewed forth in waves, much more than most demons I exorcised dispersed. I didn't worry too much about it, though. I still had to get my other arm free.

Flexing the muscles of my other arm, I pulled until the rope broke free. When it finally snapped, it was like a switch had been flipped. The others who had been frozen to the spot in surprise, came at me at once.

I jumped up from the bed and onto the warm grass. My state of undress more of a blessing than a hindrance. I couldn't imagine fighting in that tight dress and heeled shoes. I was more likely to hurt myself than anyone else.

Asmodeus stood off to the side as his lackeys came at me. One demon who had been most interested in undressing me rushed me first. His hands reached out to grab me. I ducked underneath his outstretched hands and shoved my shoulder into his stomach, knocking him off balance.

I didn't have time to exorcise them all. I'd be long dead before I could wait long enough to get them out. No, my best bet was to barrel my way through until I could get out of their little circle.

As I darted from the fallen demon's form, my eyes searched through the darkness for the vehicle we had arrived in. My gaze landed on the barely visible black SUV.

I hadn't heard them lock it, and they might not have left the keys in the car either. Who had been driving?

The potbelly and another demon came at me from both sides. They grabbed my arms and tried to pull me down, but I used their hold on me to whip myself around. My foot connected with potbelly's face, causing him to let go of my arm. I quickly shoved the talisman at the other demon shoving my aura into him without restraint.

It must have hurt like a son of a gun because he screamed so loud that it made my ears ring. I didn't wait to see him leak from his host. I ran toward the road. I could hear the last remaining two, Owen and poor Dawson, coming after me but I was faster.

The gravel road bit into my feet making me wince, but I ignored the pain as I made my way around the SUV. I jerked the door open only to frown when the keys were nowhere in sight.

"Look, I don't want to die all right."

I turned from the driver's seat where Dawson had caught up with me. He held the keys to the SUV out to me with fear in his eyes.

My eyes searched around but Owen was nowhere in sight.

That wasn't good.

Hesitating, I reached out to take the keys, only to be yanked back into the car by my hair. Kicking my legs, I grabbed onto the hands pulling me. My nails bit into the flesh making Owen grunt.

"Let me go," I struggled against his hold as he dragged me across the passenger seat, "You can't use me anyways."

"So?" Owen smirked at me when I was finally turned around enough to see him. "The boss wants to talk to you and . . ." his eyes trailed over me and I fell out of the other side of the SUV, "We've never had an angel."

"And you never will," I spat from the ground where he had dropped me.

"Keep that up and you'll wish we had just killed you," Owen reached down to grab me, but I kicked my heel out aiming for his knee.

It landed on the mark and made a sickening pop. Owen crumpled to his knees holding the one I'd hit, "Dawson, get over here!"

I hurried to my feet as Dawson made it around the front of the vehicle. With Owen still groaning on the ground, I took off toward the back. When I rounded the corner, Dawson waited on the other side.

"Do you really want to do this?" I asked him with a raised brow.

"I don't have a choice," he answered, shuffling from foot to foot, "If I let you go they'll kill me."

"Better them than me."

He thought about it for a moment, the fear clear in his eyes. Dawson thought I could kill him and had even tried to warn his friends, but truly I could only send him back to hell. Sure, I could probably destroy his very being, but it would take more energy than I was willing to use on someone like him.

It was much easier to just exorcise him.

"Grab the bitch, Dawson, or so help me you will be the next one on that bed!"

Owen's threat was enough to make up Dawson's mind. He started toward me, his eyes strangely avoiding my bra-clad chest. How the hell was he squeamish? He was about to rape me with his friends. He'd have had to see a whole lot more of me than this!

"I really don't want to do this with you, Dawson," I tried once more, "You seem like you are just in over your head. I could give you a break if you just let me go."

Dawson shook his head, determination filling his face. So much for instilling fear in the masses.

But he never made it to me. Tires squealed and in a blink of an eye, Dawson was turned into a demon pancake.

A large truck pinned him to the SUV, his hand closest to me the only thing I could see. It twitched and even tried to reach out, but he was firmly caught between the two vehicles.

"Come on!" Sid's voice called out the window of the truck. I wasted no time opening the door and jumping inside.

Sid backed the truck up and hit the gas hard enough to make gravel fly in the air. I turned to Sid. "How'd you find me?"

His brows furrowed, but his gaze stayed firmly on the road as he said, "I followed you."

"But why? You didn't help me back at the bar. Why come to my rescue now? And way to wait until the last minute."

"I apologize for that. I didn't realize you didn't have any backup with you," he smacked the steering wheel and growled, "Damn it, Mary. Why didn't you take the cops with you?"

"I couldn't have them trailing me," I explained crossing my arms over my chest.

The way my breasts pushed up reminded me how much skin I was showing. Usually, being nude didn't bother me but for some reason being so close to Sid gave me the sudden urge to hide.

Sid shook his head, "You aren't invincible, Mary. They could have killed you."

"But they didn't."

"And if I hadn't been there?" his eyes finally landed on me and then darted back to the road.

"Then I would have figured it out," I shrugged a shoulder and then said, "Why won't you look at me?"

"Fuck," Sid suddenly pulled over and he threw the car in park.

"What are you doing?" I asked as he turned in his seat to dig around in the back seat. When he righted himself, he tossed me a jacket.

"Put that on. I can't concentrate with you like that." He started the truck again, his jaw clenched tight.

I pulled the jacket on and was engulfed by his scent. The weird feeling I usually had when around Sid came back with a vengeance. Before tonight I hadn't known what it was, but now it was quite clear.

I wanted Sid.

14

I ASKED SID TO take me to my house. I don't know how he knew how to get there without me giving him directions, but I put it in the back of my mind to ask later.

Tonight had sucked big time.

It was after three, meaning the sign at Madame Serena's had long been turned off. It also meant it was the second time I'd come home with demon aura all over me.

The stink of demons was a never-ending thing. Like a prostitute, I was constantly washing, but never felt truly clean.

Sometimes I wondered if I'd ever be the way I was before. Happy and carefree. With Ramiel by my side, I hadn't wanted for anything.

But, now? I didn't see how that would ever be possible.

"Do you want me to come in with you?"

Sid's voice made me smile. "No, that's okay. I think you've played hero enough for one night."

He smirked at my words, "I'm no hero, and really it's no trouble. It would make me feel better to see you safe and sound behind a locked door."

"All right, then. To make you feel better," I hopped out of the truck cab and onto the concrete road. The rough ground reminded me that I'd lost a pair of shoes tonight as well. Not that I'd ever wear them again if I could help it.

Trisha was not going to be pleased.

Thinking of my assistant also brought my broken phone to mind.

"Crap."

"What is it? Are you all right?" Sid hurried around the truck and held his hands out as he looked me over.

"I need to check in with Trisha, but my phone got shattered, not to mention, it's still behind your bar."

"No, it's not."

I tilted my head sideways. "Huh?"

"No, it's not," he repeated as he reached into his back pocket and withdrew my phone.

Quickly taking it from him, I frowned at the cracked screen. I tried to turn it on but the screen just flickered. "Well, it was a nice thought, but it's pretty useless now."

Giving a depressed sigh, I tugged the jacket more firmly around me and moved toward the door to my office.

Walking up the stairs, I was acutely aware of Sid behind me. What was he thinking? Could he see my butt below the hem his jacket?

The fact that I even cared was peculiar to me. I had never been prudish about my body. I was an animal. He was an animal. It's not like it was anything he hadn't seen before.

My rambling thoughts were interrupted by Sid stopping behind me with an aggravated groan.

Half turning, I asked, "What is it? Changing your mind?"

Shaking his head, Sid crossed his arms over his chest and stared hard at the stairs. "I need to walk in front of you."

My brows furrowed at his words. "Why?"

"Seriously?" his eyes met mine, the heat there zeroing in on me. "I can see everything from down here."

"I'd think you'd be happy to get such a view. You're always going on about getting me naked. This will be the closest you get to it," I cocked a hip to the side and gave him a challenging glare.

That caught his attention. He took the steps between us two at a time until he was just below me. His face inches from my mine, I could feel his breath on my lips.

Sid was so close that I thought he might kiss me, but the next words out of his mouth quickly squashed that thought.

"If you think I'm even thinking about that right now after they almost raped you, then you don't know me at all."

He shoved past me and waited for me at the top of the stairs. Stunned by his words, I frowned as I caught up to him.

Unlocking the door, I flipped the light on and ushered him inside. He moved into the room like he owned the place, his eyes scanned the lackluster office supplies and couch.

I followed behind him as he crossed the reception area and went to my office door. "Is this your office?"

He didn't wait for me to answer. He opened the door and strolled right in. I leaned against the doorframe as I watched him take the room in.

Leaning against the edge of my desk, Sid gave me a forced smile, "I like it."

Laughing at his attempts to be nice, I pushed off the door, "It's a dump."

"Not if you live here."

I ignored his half-hearted attempt to flirt with me and moved to the closet, which was still a disorganized mess from Trisha dressing me earlier. Pulling Sid's jacket off, I missed the smell of him around me instantly.

Shaking the thought away, I pulled the first shirt I found over my head and unsnapped my bra with a sigh. "Remind me that I need to have God smite whatever bastard invented bras. Really, they have no purpose but to torture women."

"You got that right," Sid commented, his eyes zeroing in on my chest where my hardened nipples poked against the material of my shirt.

Crossing my arms over my chest, I glared. "Stop that."

"Stop what?" his eyes met mine and my face flushed.

"Staring at me."

Sid cocked his head to the side. "It's never bothered you before."

Turning my back on him, I grabbed a pair of sweatpants and dragged them over my hips. "Well, it does now."

"Oh, I see."

Sid's teasing tone made me spin back around. "What?" I eyeballed him. The smug expression on his face made my hand itch to slap it off.

"They made you feel something," Sid pointed at my chest.

"No, they didn't," I scoffed and brushed a hair behind my ear as I moved to my desk. I jerked the drawer open and pulled out my gun and sat it on the desk.

"Yes, they did," Sid slid along the edge of the desk until he was next to me. "Admit it. The self-righteous angel is more human than she thought."

"You're full of it," I tried to bypass him but he caught my arm and tugged me toward him.

"Then, tell me. How did you fool them?" his eyes dipped down to my lips and then back up.

"What do you mean?"

"He would have been able to tell right away that you weren't a virgin. So how did you do it?" The intensity in his gaze made me squirm.

"I didn't need to pretend," I stated and then pulled away from him and asked, "How do you know so much about it anyways?"

"I own a bar full of demons, they talk. Not well, but a thing or two does come my way," he pushed off the desk and stepped toward me, "Now stop dodging the question."

"I'm not dodging. I told you. I didn't have to fool them."

"No. You've got to be joking," he shook his head and laughed.

"I don't see how it's funny," I frowned.

Sid closed in on me his hands circling my waist and I didn't think to stop him. "You're right. It's not funny. It's damn hilarious."

"No, it's not."

"It is to me. I've spent all this time wondering what kind of guy had to have rocked your world so hard up there that you wouldn't give me the time of day and it wasn't that at all!"

I didn't like where he was going with this. Sure, I was a virgin but it wasn't a big deal. Most angels were. It just wasn't a priority up there. Not like it was down on earth.

"So, now you know," I shrugged and began to move away from him, but he held onto me. "What now?" I asked meeting his eyes.

"Now, I'm going to do what I've wanted to do since the first time I laid eyes on you," Sid's hands came up to cup my face, his fingers stroking the lines of my hair.

A tingle shot through me, and I had a feeling I knew what he wanted to do. The problem was I couldn't think of a reason to tell him no.

Call it curiosity, or that Sid was right and the demons had gotten to me, which made me feel things I wouldn't normally, but right now I wanted Sid to kiss me.

And I got my wish.

His lips were soft against mine. I didn't know what I expected them to be. I'd never been kissed before. It was obvious by how I was frozen to the spot that I had no idea what I was doing.

I kept my eyes open and watched his face. His eyes were closed; his long lashes brushed his cheeks. After a moment of our lips pressed together, his eyes fluttered open.

The gold that surrounded the center of his eyes shimmered in the green of his eyes. This close they were really something special. I didn't know why I hadn't thought to get this close to him sooner.

No sooner had I thought it than the kiss ended.

"You're frowning. You're not supposed to be frowning when I kiss you," Sid sighed and dropped his hands from my face. Instantly, I missed the warmth of his touch.

"Geez," he ran a hand through his hair. "Here I was thinking you were feeling it too and I'm just as bad as those guys. I'm sorry, Mary," he turned on his heel, but I caught his arm.

"Wait."

189

Sid glanced down at where I was holding onto him and I chewed on my lower lip. What was I going to say? I hadn't thought that far through it. I just knew I didn't want him to leave.

"You're not like them at all," I tried to reassure him, but when he only frowned harder I realized I was doing a piss poor job.

"I mean," I stared down at the ground and then up to him. "You're right. They made me feel things and I'm not too happy about it," especially since some of those things were already happening, not that I was going to tell him that.

"Okay?" Sid drew out, cocking a brow at me.

"And I might not be completely against you kissing me," my face heated as I added with a sigh, "I just don't know how to do this."

My admission got me the first real smile I had gotten from Sid all night. Dimples and all. He tucked his hands into the pocket of his sinfully-tight jeans and moved closer to me.

"You know I'd be happy to teach you," his words were soft as if telling me a secret.

Licking my lips, I breathed out, "Okay."

This time he took it slower. Sid's hands curled around my hips pressing my front to his. The material of my shirt brushed against my nipples as it made contact with the hard planes of his chest. It caused a delightful twinge between my thighs.

"So, when someone kisses you," Sid started, his head dipping down until his lips hovered over mine, "You usually close your eyes."

"Why?"

One of his hands came up to brush my hair away from my face and then it wrapped around the back of my neck. "Because you won't think so much. You focus on the feeling, not what the other person is doing. Do you think you could do that, angel?"

"Do what?"

"Give yourself over to me?" his mouth was teasing mine now and I gulped.

"Oh, yes."

"Good, because when I take you, I won't be letting you go," and then his mouth was on mine.

Unlike the first kiss, which was just a pressing of mouths, Sid devoured me. His lips captured mine, and his tongue sought out the inside of my mouth.

Curious. It was the only word I could use to describe having someone else's tongue inside my mouth. I wasn't sure why humans liked it, the slipping and sliding of saliva swapping between each other's mouths.

It wasn't until Sid pulled my tongue into his mouth and sucked on it that I realized what the big deal was about. A shock wave of need shot through me and settled between my legs.

Hot. I felt so hot down there.

My hands came up to grip the back of his head, my fingers tangling in his hair. I arched up onto my tiptoes trying to push myself closer to him.

Sid's hands moved from my waist and neck and lifted me by my butt. My legs instinctively wrapped around his waist as he moved us over to the sofa bed which was still pulled out.

Laying me down on the bed, he pressed his chest to mine. My legs tightened around him, the need in me so intense I felt like I might explode. Then, when I thought I couldn't take anymore, Sid's hand slipped beneath my shirt and cupped my breast.

My back curved and I broke the kiss to let out a long moan. His thumb rubbed across the tip as his mouth found the spot where my neck and shoulder met.

So many sensations went through me and I couldn't keep up with them. My mind was clouded. I couldn't think. I couldn't breathe.

Then, I wasn't in my office anymore with Sid above me. I lay across an altar surrounded on all sides, so much pain, and so much anguish. I couldn't take it anymore. I just wanted it to stop.

"Stop!" I shouted shoving Sid from me and across the room. He flew into the desk with a hard thud. His hand rubbed the back of his head, confusion clouding his face.

"Crap. Sid, I'm sorry," I jumped up from the bed and knelt at his side, "Did I hurt you?"

"Just a bit," Sid groaned as he got up, "No worries, angel. It was my fault. Too much too fast."

"No. No," I placed my hands under his arms to help him up, "It was all me. I'm just not all there sometimes."

Sid gave me a sad smile, "It's those scars on your back, isn't it?"

Automatically, my hand reached up to touch them but I stopped myself. Looking down at the ground, I didn't answer.

"You don't have to tell me. But one day I'd like to know what happened," his hand came up beneath my chin and tilted my face up to his, "To know how someone as pure and good as you got stuck on this piece of crap plane."

I laughed bitterly, "I'm not so pure anymore."

"Still, I'd like to know."

I nodded my head, not really agreeing to tell him. It wasn't something I had told anyone. Not completely. Not even Adara knew the whole story.

"I'd better call Trisha before she freaks out more than she already is," I stepped aside, silently asking him to leave.

Taking the hint, Sid made his way over to the door. Before he exited he turned to me, "Be careful, Mary. There are people that would miss you if you were gone." Then he was gone.

I stood in my empty office for a moment trying to come to terms with what had just happened. A slow smile spread across my face.

I'd had my first kiss. I touched my lips and found they were swollen and tingly. Who knew such an act would cause so many hormones to go wild? No wonder the humans wanted to do it so much.

I sort of giggled and half-skipped to the landline. We only had it for business reasons. Both Trisha and I had cell phones. Or well, I'd had one. Not so much anymore.

In this case, having a land-line was a blessing. I quickly dialed Trisha's number and after about twenty minutes of assuring her that I wasn't dead, and that no demons had taken over my body, and yes, I was sure I was me, I hung up.

Looking longingly at my bed, I sighed. Finally time for some shut eye. Picking up my gun, I collapsed on the bed.

Not bothering to turn out the light, I snuggled up to my gun. I had no problem shooting the next person that walked through that door. I might be an angel, but there was only so much a sleep-deprived person could handle.

15

A MAC TRUCK HAD to have hit me last night. There was no other explanation as to why I hurt so much.

I knew it wasn't true, though. I'd been there the entire time, but it'd been a while since I'd actually had to fight anyone. Usually, I was the one with the upper hand. Last night took me by surprise. It had hog-tied me and took me to dinner.

Of course, it also tried to deflower me in the name of a demon master, and that was something I was trying to forget.

With everything that happened last night, the demons, Sid, I hadn't taken a shower before I'd crashed. That explained why I felt like crap.

Demons were nasty buggers that leaked all over everyone without even knowing it. Have a bad day? A mysterious bad mood or a headache suddenly comes on? Chalk that up to coming in contact with a demon.

Which is why I always showered after a job. I didn't need their stink weighing me down. I had enough of my own.

As the hot water sprayed over me, I let out a groan. I could stay in here forever. But I knew I couldn't.

I promised Trisha I'd call her this morning and give her all the details of what went down after I'd been taken. That was not a conversation I was looking forward to.

Ugh. I rubbed the back of my neck, trying to get the heavy feeling off me.

I couldn't remember the last time I'd faced so many demons at once. The normal weight of encountering a demon seemed to be tenfold this time. God knew it wasn't just from that piece of crap Willy. Maybe it was because of Asmodeus?

My body shook from the mention of his name. What the hell was that?

He wasn't even here and just thinking of him caused my body to react. Were his powers so prevalent that he could affect someone long after they were out of his presence?

If so, then having him in the human realm would be a huge no-no. Who knew what havoc he would wreak with that kind of power?

And if I knew demons, and I did, then he wouldn't just feed enough to survive. No. He'd gorge himself on the city of Los Angeles and then move on to the rest of the state, and if not kept in check, eventually the world.

No one would be the wiser, either. They would be just like the rest of his victims, happy to die with a smile on their faces.

Just as I started to soap my hair, the phone in my office rang. Growling at the timing, I jumped from the shower, not bothering to grab a towel and darted into the other room.

Grabbing the phone off the hook, I snapped, "What?"

"Mary?" Sid's voice made the irritation in me dissipate and in its place was panic.

"Uh, Sid. Hi," I rolled my eyes at the awkwardness in my voice. What was I, a teenage girl?

"Hey," he responded back not seeming to notice my fumble.

He didn't say anything else after that and the soap in my hair was beginning to drip down my face so I said, "Did you need something?"

"Oh, yeah," Sid quickly replied, "I was calling to see how you were doing?"

A slight smile crept up my face at his words, "I could be better. I was just washing last night's demons off when you called."

There was a pause and then Sid asked, "So, you're naked then? Right this second you have no clothes on?"

I couldn't help but giggle at his question, "You have problems, you know that, right?"

"So I've been told," the smile in his voice made me grin even more.

"Is that all you called for? To see how I'm doing? You could have just waited until later. Not at . . ." I glanced at the clock. Noon? Really? I had slept longer than I thought, "Okay, so it's later than I thought, but really, that's all you wanted?"

Sid gave a short laugh and then cleared his throat, "Actually, I have some information about your demon lovers."

I snorted, "Last time I checked, trying to sacrifice me was not on my list of qualities I want in a lover."

"Then, what is?" Sid jumped in then added, "No, never mind. I'm getting off topic. Can we meet? It's easier to talk in person, and right now I really can't get the image of what you look like naked out of my mind."

My face heated to a scorching temperature and I was thankful he couldn't see it. Lord, what was wrong with me?

"Yeah, just let me finish cleaning up and then I'm all yours," I flushed at the implication of what I had just said, but didn't try to correct myself.

Sid thankfully didn't comment about it. "Want me to come to the office or do you want to come here?"

The bar was probably deserted at this time of day, which would make us completely alone. The last time we were alone, things had gotten more intense than I'd been ready for.

No. I definitely shouldn't be alone with him.

At that thought my stomach rumbled, telling me I hadn't eaten since lunch yesterday. "Actually, how about we meet at Peggy's Diner? I'm starving."

"Sounds good to me. I'll meet you there in say . . . twenty?"

My hand went to the soap that had dried in my hair and I grimaced. I'd have to do it all over again, "Let's make it forty."

"Okay, see you then."

"Bye," hanging up the phone I frowned at it. What could Sid have to tell me? It hadn't even been a day since my last encounter with the demons; things couldn't have changed that quickly, right?

I could only hope that Sid had been lying and had really just wanted an excuse to see me. The thought made me happier than I wanted to admit.

* * *

PEGGY'S DINER WAS JUST off the interstate near Glendale. It was a bit of a drive, but it had the best burgers in the city.

Apprehension filled me as the fifties-style diner came into view. I hadn't expected to see Sid this soon after our encounter. How would I act around him? Was he expecting me to kiss him when I got there?

Thankfully, when I walked in Sid had already made the decision for me. He waved an arm at me from a booth near the back.

Complete with a jukebox and red plastic chairs, the only thing Peggy's was missing was poodle skirts.

I smiled as I remembered when Trisha had made me watch Grease. The hot rods mixed with musical numbers had been an interesting experience. Though, the last song in it made no sense to me. If the car could fly, why didn't Danny just fly to the finish line?

Shaking my head, I cleared the thought of leather pants and singing out of my head, and focused on the man in front of me.

Sid, as usual, looked good enough to eat. In the bright diner's light, I could see the streaks of lighter brown through his almost black hair. He'd opted for a buttoned-down shirt this time with the sleeves rolled up to the elbows so his tattoos were peeking out beyond the edges. I'd never seen him so cleaned up before.

The dimple in his cheek waved hello as I slid into the seat across from him. A warm feeling settled between my thighs, and I forced myself to pick up the slightly sticky menu so I could get a grip on my hormones.

"So, do you come here often?" Sid asked, picking up his own menu.

"Mhmm," I kept my eyes on the menu, not trusting myself not to say something stupid.

A hand came out from behind my menu and pulled it down until Sid's eyes met mine. His eyes crinkled around the edges, and his frown set me on edge.

"What's up, angel? It's not like you to be so quiet."

"Nothing," I said quickly, trying to pull my menu back up, but his hand slapped down on it keeping it firmly against the table.

Before he could ask me any more, a waitress—bless her—came up to the table. Aggie was my usual waitress when I came to Peggy's, and I knew her almost as well as Trisha.

"Hey, Aggie," I smiled up at her, "How are the grandchildren?"

Aggie ruffled her short gray hair and scowled, "Oh, you know, still raising hell. That mama of theirs might have been raised by me, but she doesn't seem to know that sometimes a kid needs a talkin' to and sometimes they just need a good butt-whoppin'."

We chuckled for a moment and then Aggie's eyes fell on Sid. She placed a hand on the back of her hip and looked between us, "Why, Mary, you didn't tell me you had a boyfriend."

"He's not my—"

"Oh, yeah," Sid cut me off grabbing my hands across the table, "We've been together for a while now, haven't we, angel?"

His eyes sent me a silent challenge, all the while his thumb rubbed circles along my hand. Tiny tingles shot through me and I bit my lip to force back the need to correct him.

Why he wanted to pretend we were dating was beyond me, but if it would keep him touching me I was all for it.

I leaned forward in my seat and gripped his hands tighter. His eyes widened, probably because I didn't immediately remove his hands from mine. It made my own lips tick up a bit.

"Oh, yes, Aggie. This delicious piece of man meat really got me good. I just can't keep my hands off of his massive cock."

Sid made a choking sound while Aggie just laughed, "Well, honey. I can't say I blame ya. If I had a man like that I'd never get dressed again!"

Letting go of one of his hands, but not breaking eye contact with Sid, I handed the menus to Aggie, "Two of the usual's."

"You got it," she took the menus without jotting anything down, "You kids keep it PG. We've got little ones in here. At least above the table," Aggie winked.

As she wandered off, I withdrew my hands and started laughing. Sid was still frozen in shock. His mouth hung slightly open and he was making weird gulping noises.

"Are you okay?" I asked, waving my hand in front of his face. "Do you need something to drink? I can call Aggie back?" I half stood up from the table to wave her down when Sid's hand clamped down on mine.

"Don't you dare," the growl that rumbled from him only made me laugh more.

"Hey, you started this game. Don't blame me if you can't finish it," I warned, pointing a finger at him.

"Well, most *humans* know not to say the word cock in public," his face flushed as he said it, "Where did you even learn that word from anyways? Isn't it too dirty of a word for an angel to know?"

"From Trisha, of course," I shrugged, "Apparently, there are all kinds of things like that on the Internet. Speaking of Trisha, she should have called me by now," I pulled out the old flip-phone I'd found in a drawer at the office and checked the screen. Nope. No calls, no texts, nothing.

Maybe she slept in late too?

Shrugging it off, I turned back to Sid. "So, what's this information you have for me?"

Sid shifted in his seat, suddenly not joking around anymore. His eyes looked off to the side and a guilty expression covered his face.

"Come on, Sid. Spill. I don't have all day. Trisha is sure to start blowing up my phone any minute. This is your time to shine."

My prodding had the opposite effect. Instead of answering right away, he seemed to sink further into his seat. The frown on his face deepened.

"Sidney?" I said this time my voice less aggressive, "What is it?"

"I don't know how to tell you this, Mary, but I'm just going to come out and say it," Sid said, finally looking me in the eye. Whenever he called me Mary—and not angel—I knew he was being serious. Whatever he had to tell me was bad.

"It can't be that bad. It's not like you killed anyone?" I quirked a brow at him. "Did you?"

Before he could answer my phone rang. Expecting it to be Trisha, I picked it up and was annoyed to see Sergeant Thompson's name flash over the screen.

"It's barely been twelve hours. This had better be good," I answered not bothering with pleasantries.

"It's important. We got a tip that the guys we've been hunting will be trying again tonight. We need you to get back out there," Thompson's voice was gruff but had a weird twinge to it that I didn't like.

"Thompson, I almost died last night. I need a break," I sighed and then argued, "Whoever your tipster is, they lied. They won't try again until the next cycle of the moon so we are good for at least—"

"Mary," Thompson cut me off with a seriousness that made me pause, "It's Trisha."

16

I BOLTED OUT OF the diner without a word to Sid. When I got to the parking lot I remembered I'd taken the bus here.

"Shit!"

Footsteps pounded on the concrete behind me, and I spun around to meet Sid's worried face, "Give me your keys."

"What?" His brow crinkled. "Why?"

"I need . . . I need your keys. I've got to go," I held my hand out, gesturing for him to hand them over.

To my frustration, he didn't give them to me. Instead, he placed his hand on my shoulders and said in a soft soothing voice, "Calm down. Tell me what happened."

I jerked away from him making his hands fall from my shoulders, "I don't want to calm down!" I grabbed at my hair and tugged tight until the pain made my heart stop thundering in my chest, "They have Trisha and it's my fault," gritting my teeth, I glared at Sid, "I should have killed the bastards when I had the chance."

Sid's expression didn't change to surprise or even worry. In fact, the guilty look from before came back. Then it dawned on me.

"You knew!" I pointed an accusing finger at him, "That's what you were trying to tell me back at the diner. You knew they'd taken her."

He held his hands up and took a step back from me. "Look, I'm just the messenger. They wanted to make sure that you got the message in case the cops decided not to tell you."

"But why would they tell you?"

Shrugging, Sid dug into his pocket and pulled his keys out. "I own the bar where you met. Obviously, they thought we knew each other."

I reached a hand out to take the keys but he pulled them out of my reach, "No way. I'm driving. You don't even have a license. Besides, I feel partly responsible for Trisha being taken anyways."

"It's not your fault," I shook my head, "I shouldn't have let her get involved in any of this. If anyone's to blame, it's me."

Sid didn't argue with me as he led me over to his truck. The front of it didn't have a scratch on it, no sign that he'd plowed over Dawson last night. The thought of the demons made my blood boil.

"Where are we going?" Sid asked, prepped and ready to go.

"A warehouse just outside of town. About ten minutes from here," I dragged my seat belt on with an angry click, "Thompson said he'd meet me there."

"You got it, angel," putting the truck into gear, Sid peeled out of the diner's parking lot and onto the street.

I didn't know what I was going to do if I showed up and they'd already hurt Trisha. But I did know that if she wasn't alive when I arrived, hell would be the least of their worries.

They were going to pay. Every single one of them.

* * *

As far as abandoned warehouses went, this one was in pretty good shape. Sid parked on the street a ways away from it, and turned to me.

"Are you sure about this, angel?" his brow quirked in question, "They almost got you last night, and you are still recovering from that."

I shook my head, "I don't have a choice. I can't just let them have her."

"But the cops are here," he gestured to a few unmarked cars that were not fooling anyone. I could see Thompson from where we sat, talking to a few of his men as they strapped on their bullet-proof vests.

"Their guns won't work here. Not unless they are blessed, and I highly doubt that. But, hopefully, they will be enough of a distraction that I can get Trisha out safely."

"All right, if you are sure," he reached over me to open the glove compartment. "You are going to need some protection."

Sid pulled out a silver and brown gun—I couldn't place the type. He popped a magazine into the bottom. Turning it around, he offered the butt of it to me. "Here. There are eight bullets in there, blessed by a priest just recently."

"Thanks. That's all I need," eight bullets were more than enough. If I needed anymore, I'd be dead anyways.

I popped the door open but paused. Turning back in the seat, I grabbed Sid by the collar of his shirt and pressed my lips to his.

At first, he didn't respond and then his hands came up and cupped my face. I licked across his lips, and to my gratitude, he opened them, letting me get a taste. Before it could get too intense, I let go of his collar and released his mouth.

"Thanks," I smiled at him as I hopped out of the truck and headed toward the cops that were waiting for me with knowing grins on their faces.

"Not your boyfriend, right?" Thompson commented, but I ignored him.

Pointing the gun Sid had given me down to the ground, I looked around. There were a dozen officers. It wouldn't be enough.

Not if the demons had gotten reinforcements. One demon would need five times as many humans to take them down.

Luckily, they had me.

"So the plan is—" Thompson started, but I cut him off.

"I'm going in alone. Then, when I give the signal you come in like the cavalry you are."

Thompson frowned at my plan, "Now hold on a minute. We can't just let you go in there by yourself. You said so yourself. They almost killed you last night."

"But, it's me they want," I pointed out, "If I come in there guns blazing, with all of you, they might take off *with* Trisha."

The sergeant tried to argue with me again, but I stopped him with a shake of my head, "You haven't met these guys, Thompson. You don't know them like I do. They won't hesitate to kill her the moment you guys show your faces."

"Fine," Thompson crossed his arms over his large chest and then nodded toward my gun, "the moment things get hairy, you shoot that piece you got from your boyfriend and we'll come running."

"How do you know I got it from him?" I glanced down at the gun in my hand.

Thompson smirked, "Because, there's no way a woman with your hands would buy a piece like that without male input."

Shaking my head, I couldn't help but smile. Men. Human, demon, or angelic they were all the same.

As I made my way toward the warehouse my grin faded. I could feel them, even from here. There were more demons than last time, that was for sure.

I couldn't count how many. My powers didn't work that way, but I knew that if I went in the building there was a good chance that neither Trisha nor I would come out alive.

Shaking off my nerves, I held the gun with both hands and inched toward the back side of the building. Going through the front was what they wanted. I wasn't going to give them that.

Sliding my back against the metal of the warehouse, I hissed. The heat of the sun had turned the siding into molten lava and it burned my back through my shirt.

Making sure not to touch the side again, I moved down the side until I found a window where I could peek inside. There were boxes and shelves in the way. I couldn't see any further in.

I pushed at the window and was surprised to find it unlocked. As nice as the warehouse was, I'd have expected tighter security over its openings.

Shrugging it off, I moved as quietly as I could until I was through the window and I landed with a small noise on the concrete floor.

Glancing around, I was thankful that I was mostly surrounded by other boxes and shelves. There weren't any demons waiting in the shadows ready to pop out at me.

My feet were soundless as I slowly made my way down the aisle between two shelves. The smell of musty cardboard filled my nose as I took every inch of my surroundings in.

It was too quiet.

Pressing my back to the shelf, I rounded its corner until I could peek around the edge. On the other side were more shelves and boxes.

Frowning, I was tired of not getting any action. This was supposed to be a rescue, but how could I rescue anyone if I couldn't find them?

I got to the end of the next row and froze as I came face-to-face with the barrel of a gun.

On the other side of that gun was Owen, smiling like the cat that ate the canary, "Look what I found. An angel fallen from her cloud. All alone and in need of comfort."

Curling my lip up into a snarl, I growled, "I'm not anyone's fallen angel, and I would rather get comfort from a rattlesnake than you."

Owen smiled at my words, "You hold onto that spirit, little angel. I'll want that spirit when I'm taking you," he leered over me as if I were wearing a slinky nightgown and not jeans and a t-shirt.

"Stop messing with her, Owen," Asmodeus' voice called out from beyond the shelves, "Bring our guest to me. Your fellow brothers' wish to meet her."

I closed my eyes against the rush of heat that filled my body. Damn him and his voice. The first thing I was going to do was shoot out his tongue. Then we'd see who the master was.

With my plan firmly in place, I let Owen lead me through the maze of shelves. He hadn't asked for my gun, but since he was a demon he probably thought I wouldn't have blessed bullets.

Good thing for dumb demons.

We rounded the final corner and came into an open area. There were more shelves and boxes around the edges of the warehouse but in the center, sitting in a metal fold out chair, was Asmodeus.

He sat with one leg crossed over the other, his arms lying along the tops of his thighs. His hair was slicked back as before, but he didn't wear a suit this time.

He still wore the same black dress-pants, but the jacket was missing and his sleeves were rolled up to his elbows. The first few buttons of the shirt were undone showing the pale skin beneath.

All in all, if he hadn't been a demon trying to kill my friend, I'd have been easily attracted to him. But since he was the demon of lust, I supposed in any form he would seem appealing. While my brain was telling me I hated him, my body—the traitorous bastard that it was—didn't agree.

"Hello, lovely. So nice to see you again," Asmodeus greeted with a full-toothed grin. The moment I came into his presence that burning need from before started inside of me.

It made me pause mid-step, but Owen shoved me from behind forcing me to keep walking. Glaring at him over my shoulder, I started moving again. Not because he wanted me to, but because of what lay in the middle of the room.

Ignoring the pulsating feeling coming from between my thighs, my attention was only on Trisha. She was bound to the bed in the center of the room, tied down to the bed as I had been before. Unlike me though, she thankfully still had all her clothing on. Thank God for her fashion sense. The thick skirt and multi-layered top underneath a corset would have made hard work for them.

The good news? They hadn't touched her yet. The bad news? Things were about to get ugly.

17

THE SIGHT OF TRISHA bound to the bed made my stomach sick. It wasn't something I'd ever wanted to see happen to her. And I promised it would never happen again.

If we got out of here alive.

"Mary!" Trisha cried out from where she struggled against the ropes. But I knew it was useless. She was only eighteen and human at that.

In this moment, there was nothing I wouldn't give to trade places with her, but it was silly to pray for it. No one was listening. At least if the big guy was he hadn't felt so inclined to answer any of my prayers since I'd left.

He probably thought he was teaching me a lesson. Inwardly, I scoffed at the idea. The bigger picture had always been the deal, but the longer I stayed on earth the more I felt like the bigger picture was do-what-you're-told-or-no-one-will-help-you-when-you get fucked.

Which meant I was on my own.

"Hey, Trisha. Comfortable?" I asked with a reassuring smile, trying to make light of the situation.

"Not particularly," she grimaced and shook her head, "Remind me never to complain about our lumpy couch again."

"As touching as this reunion is," Asmodeus stood from his chair and stepped between us, "I believe we have some business to attend to."

My eyes narrowed on the demon before me, my hand tightening around the butt of Sid's gun, "What do you want?"

I'd learned it was easiest to get straight to the point with bad guys. Demons or humans all wanted to screw you over, so might as well know what you were getting screwed for.

"Now, don't ruin all the fun. We are just getting started," Asmodeus pouted, an expression that should have looked childish on him, but just added to his appealing looks. It had to be some kind of demon mojo. There was no way this guy could be that attractive.

Other demon's auras were potent, easy to spot when my veil was down, but even with it up this guy pushed against my radar. But not in the way I'd expected.

He moved across the room, almost floating. His feet didn't make a sound as they skimmed the ground. Unnerving.

The demon stopped in front of a table off to the side of the bed. On top of it were several items, none of which were pleasant.

Among them was a long metal rod with a pointed tip and a wooden handle. Asmodeus let his fingers dance over it before moving them along to the next one. This one was a long knife, almost a sword with a curved edge. His hand paused on it and then he picked it up. He turned from the table.

"You know, I've heard about you," he pointed the sword at me with a devious grin.

"Oh, really?"

"Oh, yes," he nodded with enthusiasm. "The angel who fell from heaven to save her beloved only to be captured by nasty demons," he tut-tutted at me, "Not a very happy story."

"Mary?" my eyes flickered over to Trisha who was looking between Asmodeus and me. I could see the confusion there. She hadn't quite gotten the fact that I was the angel he was talking about.

"Is what he's saying true?"

Asmodeus laughed at her question, the rest of his minions joining in. He swiped the knife across the air and just like that they silenced. "Dear child, you really don't know what you have gotten into, do you?"

If looks could kill Trisha would have skewered Asmodeus and popped him over a fire to burn. I couldn't help but feel a bit of pride. That's my girl.

Before I could answer her, Asmodeus continued, "Well, let me fill in the blanks for you about your current employer."

He practically skipped across the room and splayed himself next to her on the bed. Trisha inched away from him as much as the restraints allowed her. If Asmodeus cared he didn't mention it. His eyes were too focused on me.

"You see," he waved the knife back and forth in the air, "your dear employer here is not as human as she would lead you to believe. Did you think that a mere human would be able to take down my demons like she does?"

The demon glanced back at Trisha and then glared at me, "No, only someone equally as otherworldly would be able to get in my way so often. So annoyingly," he made a face and then turned his attention back to Trisha. He laid his head on her stomach. She made a small noise but didn't move or try to shove him away.

I didn't know if he was using his power against her, but the fear in her eyes said if he was she wasn't letting it overcome her.

Asmodeus rubbed his face against the hard ridges of Trisha's corset and then sat up with a frown. "You know," he shook the knife slightly as he spoke, "I'm actually quite impressed with you."

Not looking at me, he slipped the blade between one of the front corset strings of Trisha's top. It snapped easily under the sharp edge of the blade and Trisha whimpered.

Keep him talking, Mary.

"Why's that?" I asked, taking a step closer. Owen tried to stop me but strangely Asmodeus waved him off.

"If she wants to come closer, let her. I do not fear the little angel," the twinkle in his eye made me livid, but I swallowed down my rage. *Think of Trisha, think of Trisha.*

"Anyways, like I was saying," he popped another string of the corset, "You have really impressed me. To not only live through the torturous ordeal of having your wings torn off—"

"Sawed off," I interrupted.

He paused in his actions and turned to me with a raised brow, "Really now? That's even worse. Now you have me curious," he searched me over as if trying to see the damage, "Tell me, how did that feel?"

"Like I was getting my wings sawed off," I answered, the sarcasm dripping from my words.

The demon didn't seem to care and continued popping the strings of Trisha's top, each one resulting in a noise from the young girl.

"I'd imagine it would be quite excruciating," he commented and then

226

paused, cocking his head to the side, "I, myself, have never been much for torture but just thinking of it makes me wish I had been there for myself to see you scream and beg."

I gritted my teeth and bit out, "Then I'll make sure to send you an invite the next time it happens."

This made him smile, "Look at you being all polite. When inside you are thinking about ripping me open to see what my innards look like, aren't you?"

"Actually, I was thinking of how much more attractive you'd look without your head attached to your body."

Asmodeus chuckled, "You are vicious, aren't you? Are you sure there isn't some demon in you?" he waved the knife at my midsection.

Stopping by the side of the bed, I didn't answer as I reached out to take the knife from him. Before my hand could touch the blade, he pulled it out of my reach.

"Ah, ah, ah," he shook his finger at me, "We were having such a lovely conversation. Why did you have to go and ruin it?"

"I'm just rude like that," I reached again for the knife but missed and lost my balance, ending up with Asmodeus lying next to Trisha on the bed and me half over him.

"Now, isn't this cozy."

"Just fantastic," Trisha remarked rolling her eyes. Good, I wasn't the only one who thought this guy was nuts.

"Now, no talking from the peanut gallery," Asmodeus placed the blade along Trisha's throat and watched me.

Resisting the urge to try for the knife again, I leaned back slightly, "Cut to the chase, demon. I'm tired of these games."

A glint filled his eye as he said, "Let's make a deal."

"I don't make deals with demons," was my automatic reply.

My answer only made him grin wider, "I have a feeling this one will be the exception."

Making deals with demons was a big no-no. They never ended well.

One of my past clients had made such a deal. In exchange for her soul, the demon had promised to make her famous. She had readily agreed to it and she became famous all right.

A sex tape—one taken without her knowledge— had ended up posted all over the Internet. Her friends and family, even her coworkers had seen it. She had been so humiliated that she had come to me for help.

The problem was, I hadn't been able to help her. No one could. If you didn't specify the how, when, and down to the very last minute detail, then the demons would twist your wishes to hell and back. And there wasn't a damn thing you could do about it.

I couldn't break the contract she had made. I couldn't give her her soul back. What I could do, was exorcise the demon and send him back to hell, but her soul would still end up there when she died.

Still, she had begged me to do it. That it didn't matter anymore what happened to her. So long as the demon who tricked her couldn't do it to anyone else.

I hadn't had the heart to tell her that he could come back. They usually did, but not for a while and they were usually smart enough to stay clear of me afterward.

That was why, no matter what he offered me, I would absolutely refuse. And as I got off the bed, making him frown, I firmly said, "No."

He obviously didn't believe me. The demon thought I could be persuaded, they all did. But I wasn't so easily convinced.

"Now, don't be denying me before you can hear my offer," he moved to the edge of the bed and Trisha visibly relaxed. She was doing better than most humans would have in her situation. I'd have to remember to give her hazard pay after this.

First, I'd have to get paid. Oh, the joys of living on earth.

Shaking my thoughts from my head, I narrowed my gaze on him, "I don't care what you have to offer. I'm not making a deal with you. I want Trisha and I want her now."

"Well, now you aren't playing fair," Asmodeus dipped his chin down, looking up at me beneath his lashes, "You see, I have this little problem. I need a virgin so I can come to this plane. You," he jutted the knife toward me, "were supposed to be that virgin, but we both know that won't help me at all. So," he shifted until his hand landed on Trisha's tight-clad thigh, her leg tensed at his touch, "I need her to finish the ritual and it has to be tonight, or I have to start all over again."

"Poor you," I retorted, earning me a searing glare before Asmodeus forced the look from his face and smiled up at me.

"I propose," I opened my mouth to interrupt but he placed the knife against the inside of Trisha's thigh, "Did you know that the artery here is quite lethal? Just a nick would bleed her out in minutes."

"Then why bother with me and just do it?" I dared him. "Just kill her and get it over with."

"Mary!" Trisha cried out, "What the fuck?"

"Would you rather be raped and then killed?" I yelled at her, which promptly shut her up.

"Because as you just said, she is more useful to me alive until I can complete the ritual, but I will kill her if that is what it takes to get you off my back."

"If you kill her, I will never be off your back," I challenged, "I will hunt you until judgment day, and then you will wish I had killed you now."

"Now, now. Threats are no good if I have something you want," he shook his head with a knowing smile.

"What could you possibly have that I want more than her?"

"Let me have her," he leaned in and lowered his voice, "and I'll tell you where your wings, and your friend are."

He was lying. He had to be. That's what demons did . . . offered you the world then just as you reach out to take it, they jerk it out of your reach.

"You're lying," I smiled, "You don't know where either of them are. You don't even know his name."

At my accusation, his lips curled up into an evil, self-satisfied smile, "You mean, Ramiel?"

Just hearing the name caused my throat to clench. It'd been five years since I'd seen, or heard from, my commanding officer and one-time best friend. Now I didn't even know if he was alive.

"So what? You know his name," I shrugged trying to be nonchalant, "Doesn't mean you know anything else."

"Oh, I wouldn't be so sure about that," Asmodeus countered, "demons talk, and I'm not a lower-class demon who grasps at any information I can get a hold of. Information is power, and I want it all," he splayed his fingers wide in front of him before closing them tightly.

"Well, so far all I've heard is wind because nothing you are saying is making me want to let you have her. In fact," I lifted my gun and pointed it at him, "I'm tired of talking."

Asmodeus laughed, "You think your puny weapon can hurt me? I am immortal. This shell will sustain me until I have crossed over and heal any damage that you might do," he stood from the bed and held his arms wide open, "But if you insist on making a spectacle of yourself, then by all means, take your best shot."

"Holy bullets, asshole," I smirked before I pulled the trigger.

18

THE SOUND OF ASMODEUS screaming as the bullet ripped through him was like music to my ears.

Sadly, I didn't have long to enjoy it, because not more than a second after I shot him, Owen was on me.

"You'll pay for that," he growled, trying to take the gun out of my hand, I wrenched away from him and rolled across the concrete. Aiming as soon as I was up, I shot Owen in the chest.

He crumbled to the ground like a rag doll, his essence pouring out of him and into the ground. One down, way too many to go.

I was down to six bullets, one that had been wasted on Asmodeus because he hadn't left his host. He sat next to the bed clutching the wound in his chest.

"Where the hell are those cops?" I gritted my teeth, my eyes darting around me as the demons closed in. They should have been here by now. Two shots were plenty enough warning to let them know I needed them. Laughter from Asmodeus made my head jerk toward him.

"Your pathetic backup is not coming," he coughed and wheezed. I must have hit a lung. Good. I hoped it hurt like a bitch.

"What happened to them?" I asked, pointing my gun at the closest demon, making him hesitate, "What'd you do?"

"It's not what I did," he laughed and then groaned, "but what your beloved Sidney has done."

"Sidney?" my eyebrows rose high on my forehead, "What does he have to do with any of this?"

The demons quickly circled me, laughing together as if there were some inside joke I was not privy to. In my frustration, I squeezed the trigger too tight and shot the nearest demon in the shoulder causing him to fall to his knees. He groaned, but didn't spill out of his host.

Damn. I'd missed the heart.

Demons weren't easily killed and could be exorcised from a distance with holy bullets, but you had to get them in the heart or head of the host. The blessed metal kept the demon from healing his body and thus killing the host.

I'd just wasted a bullet. It pissed me off.

I aimed at the next demon that happened to be the potbelly demon from the clearing. Giving a nasty grin, I didn't have to aim much and got him right in his bulbous head.

The darkness poured out of him and I laughed. It sounded maniacal even to me. But what Asmodeus said next really caused the rage to fill me.

"Sidney has been playing you a fool," he chuckled and eased up from the ground, the hole still dripping blood.

"I don't know what you are talking about."

Asmodeus held onto the footboard of the bed and smiled, "he's been working for me this whole time."

"Why would he do that? He's human," I asked, turning the gun back on him

"Half."

"What?"

Asmodeus' smile split into a shit-eating grin, "He's only half human. The other half is mine."

I heard his words, but it was like they didn't register in my brain. Sid was a demon. Okay, so he was half demon, but that still meant part of him was evil. It just didn't make any sense.

But it did.

When I really thought about it, it made perfect sense. He ran a bar full of demons. It explained why there was always an electric pull whenever I went into it. Even my attraction to him all screamed my-dad-is-a-sex-demon.

And I had fallen for it. The off-handed answers about getting information from his clients. The time he took that couple to the back. Even the fact that he knew I was an angel without me telling him.

All signs pointed to him being the son of the jerkwad before me. I didn't understand how I could be so stupid. So manipulated. I'd even let him . . . I let him be my first kiss.

My first kiss was taken by a demon! That thought alone made me see red. Heaving in a lung full of air, I barely registered Asmodeus coming up next to me.

"I know it hurts," he patted my shoulder, "But look at it this way, at least now you know."

"Don't touch me," I snarled, shoving his hand off of me and then pointing the gun at his head, "Don't ever touch me or my friends again."

Before I could pull the trigger the doors of the warehouse were thrown open and the LAPD poured in. "Police! Put your hands up where I can see them."

Sergeant Thompson's voice distracted me enough that Asmodeus hit me. Unlike when Owen hit me, this didn't just hurt, but it made me see stars. I fell to the ground with a groan, my gun flying across the floor.

The good thing about cops in LA was they were a shoot-first-ask-questions-later kind of group. If it hadn't been for them, Asmodeus would have been on me in seconds, but he was too busy being filled with bullets to pay me any mind.

"Mary!" Trisha called from the bed struggling against her bindings, "Come untie me."

Slowly climbing to my hands and feet, I shook off the darkness threatening to fill my head and stumbled toward Trisha. Once at the bed, I paused to catch my breath, my hands on one of the ropes.

"Why didn't you tell me you were an angel?" Trisha asked as I jerked the cord, breaking it easily.

Frowning down at her, I asked, "Do you really think this is the time to discuss this?"

"Well, it's completely destroyed my whole atheist view," she continued as I reached over her to snap the other restraint.

"You believe in demons, but not angels or God," I shook my head, "I don't get you, Trisha."

"It makes perfect sense," she argued, sitting up from the bed and rubbing her wrists, "There's enough-Mary behind you!"

I ducked in time before a demon tried to lop my head off with one of the tools that he had grabbed off the table. Turning on my heel, I shoved my talisman against his face making him scream.

Not waiting to see if he was gone, I rushed around the bed to pull at the ropes on Trisha's ankles.

"Anyways," Trisha continued, "like I was saying. There's enough bad shit in the world that it's easy to believe that supernatural forces are behind it. That being said, if God exists —"

"He does."

"Then why doesn't he stop it?" she wiggled her legs and then slid off the bed and to my side.

I shook my head, "It's complicated."

I really couldn't answer her, because I had asked myself the same question hundreds of times.

If God really loved his precious humans so much, why did he let them become so corrupted and evil? Why were children starving and people killing each other left and right?

One thing was for sure, that crap would have never gone down in heaven. There was a tight leash on everything, and everyone. Not that angels were even aware of the box they were in. No, they were happily, oblivious in their contentment.

Not me, though. Not anymore.

I knew what happened when you didn't toe the line. I'd felt the cold emptiness of not having his presence on my side. It wasn't pleasant. It was lonely. After five years, I still hadn't gotten over it.

"Come on," I grabbed Trisha's hand and led her through the crowd of fighting demons and cops. The cops might have them out-numbered, but the demons were faster and the bullets they were shooting weren't doing much of anything.

"What bothers me the most . . ." Trisha kept talking as we jumped over a fallen cop.

"Almost getting raped and sacrificed wasn't enough for you?"

She gave me a dry look and then said, ". . . no. What bothers me is that if you are an angel, are you really allowed to curse? I mean, aren't you afraid you'll go to hell when you die?"

I opened my mouth to answer her, but before I could Asmodeus' voice interrupted, "No, she's not."

Twisting around until my eyes landed on him, I frowned, "You aren't dead yet?"

"Not quite yet," he laughed and then coughed, the bullets that he had been shot with came out of his mouth and made a pinging noise as they hit the concrete.

"But to answer your question," he continued as if he wasn't about to keel over right in front of us, "Angels and demons don't have souls like humans. When we die, that's it. We're done," his gaze leveled with mine in an understanding truth.

"What?" Trisha cried out, "That's ridiculous. So, you are just gone? Done? Poof?" She made an explosion motion with her hands, "Just like that?"

I nodded sullenly.

"Well, that's not very fair."

"No, it's not," Asmodeus commented, "but if we could come to this plane, we could change all that. Couldn't we, Mary?"

"What's he talking about?" Trisha touched my shoulder, and I turned to her to explain, but that was what Asmodeus had been waiting for.

He jumped onto my back, shoving me to the ground. The weight of him pinned me down and I couldn't get him off me. Even wounded, he was still too strong.

I tried to get my talisman up to his face but he laughed and shoved my hands down to the ground beneath me. "Your silly holy magic can't help you. Now," he licked his lips with a feral growl, "shall we see what you taste like, *Muriel?*"

19

ASMODEUS WAS STILL A force to be reckoned with, even though he possessed a human.

His strength was more than I had ever experienced. His aura leaked all over me, now that I was pressed up against him.

I fought against the urges he tried to instill inside me. This guy was evil. No time for my body to get all girly on me.

Remember, Mary. Evil.

Chanting the mantra over and over in my head, I struggled against him physically and mentally. Finally, he realized I wasn't going to roll over and let him mount me like he was used to, and he let up on the power attack.

"You are more stubborn than I gave you credit for," he purred leaning in until his breath was on my face, "But why should I be surprised. You've survived hell. If I want to get to you, I'll have to change up my game."

"Good luck with that," I snarled shoving at him with my legs. Asmodeus simply planted himself on my hips so that my legs could not reach him.

Smart demon.

"So, let me think," he glanced up at the ceiling, his brow furrowing as he thought. "What makes Muriel tick? What drives her desires?"

"Sure as hell not you."

He laughed darkly, "I would think not. But maybe my son does?"

When I didn't answer and only glared at him, his grin widened, "Hit a sore spot, have I?"

"You haven't hit anything. But I will," I struggled against his grip trying to get my talisman to touch some part of him, "Once I get free."

His eyes shot to my hand with the talisman wrapped around it. "Ah, ah, ah. No playing unfair, now," Asmodeus grabbed a hold of the chain. It snapped, and he chucked it across the room.

My eyes followed it as it slid away and under the bed, "You're going to have to pay for that."

Smirking at me, he ground his hips into mine, "You can take it out in favors."

Ugh, and I thought demons were bad. Apparently the master demons were even worse.

"I'd rather die."

"That could be arranged," his eyes moved from me and I followed the direction of his gaze as it landed on the knife not a foot from us. An array of emotions crossed his face, and I knew he was trying to figure out how to keep me down and grab the knife too.

I betted he'd go for the knife. I was hoping for it.

As soon as I thought it, he let go of one of my hands to reach for it. That's when I struck.

Of course, lying on the ground with someone on top of you wasn't the easiest way to punch someone, but I did what I could.

I swung my fist and it connected with his jaw, but either my punch just didn't have the same effect it did standing up or

Asmodeus' host's jaw was made of steel, because he didn't so much as flinch. My hand, though, was another story.

Wincing at the pain radiating from it, I tried to ignore it and find another way to get him off of me since brute force wasn't going to work.

"Now," Asmodeus held up the knife with a wicked gleam, "Let's see what lies beneath that stony facade shall we?"

As he held the knife up above me, glass shattered and the demon jerked. Pieces fell from either side of Asmodeus and his eyes rolled up into the top of his head. He teetered from side to side, and I shoved him off of me and onto the ground revealing Trisha behind him.

"What would you do without me?" Trisha smiled and dropped the vase to the ground with a thump.

She offered me a hand, which I readily took, and hauled me to my feet. I stared down at Asmodeus where he lay on the ground. He wasn't moving, but that didn't mean anything.

My eyes searched around the warehouse until they fell on where my gun had gone. Or, well, Sid's gun. The thought of Sid made me prickle, but I ignored it. Beggars couldn't be choosers.

Thompson's voice called out to me as I picked up the gun, "Wiles! Stop pussy-footing around. We need to get your statement and make sure all the bodies we have are accounted for."

Twisting toward his voice, I paused. Sid stood next to Thompson, his hands in his pockets and looking as delicious as ever.

When he felt my gaze on him he glanced up. Our eyes locked for a split second before I broke contact.

A cruel fist squeezed at my heart and I swallowed hard. *You can do this, Mary. He's like any other scumbag demon.*

Taking a deep breath, I held the gun tight in my grip as I marched over to where Thompson stood with Sid, "What took you guys so long?"

Sid stiffened at my question but didn't answer. Thompson did though.

"While you were in here playing around, we were outside waiting for your signal but then at least a dozen guys came out of nowhere and attacked us," Thompson gestured toward the cars just outside the warehouse doors.

My eyes strained to see any evidence of what he said, but all I saw were bodies on the ground, "How'd you get away from them?"

Thompson smiled and clapped Sid on the shoulder, "Well, that's where your lover here comes in," I winced at the name, but didn't correct him.

"We were having a real heck of a time. Losing men in seconds when Sidney here came blazing in with some of those holy bullets you have there and took them out. Like that!" he snapped his fingers, real pride in his eyes.

"Oh really?" my gaze settled on Sid, he shifted in his spot, but didn't meet mine.

"Yeah," Thompson continued, not noticing the tension between Sid and I. "Then we high-tailed it over here when we heard your third shot. Sorry we were late. The damn bastards jumped us right before you gave the signal."

I shook my head and gave a weak smile. "Don't worry about it. We caught them. That's all that matters."

Thompson nodded and then pulled out a little notepad and began to scribble down on it. "So, Wiles, can you go around and count those who are still alive, and the bodies lying around, and make sure we got them all?" he gestured toward the room with his pen.

"Sure, Sergeant," I turned on my heel without a word to Sid, completely determined not to give into the puppy-dog eyes he had been casting my way when I wasn't looking.

The first place I went was to retrieve my talisman from under the bed. I frowned at the broken chain. It would cost a pretty penny to fix it. It looked like I had more jobs to do when I got back home.

Shoving it in my pocket, I made my way around the room, counting as I went until I ended up back where Asmodeus' body lay. He was still out cold, or dead for all I knew. But someone would have to check. It might as well be me.

With the gun pointed at his head, I began to kneel down on the ground to check him. But before I could, the voice of the one I was pretending didn't exist called my name.

"What?" I answered, standing from the ground, my eyes still firmly on the demon by my feet.

"Can we talk?" I could feel him stop behind me. The heat of his body radiated through me and made my insides curl up in pleasure. It pissed me off.

"No. We can't talk," I retorted, not turning around. I kept the gun pointed down at Asmodeus, but my vision began to blur.

Fuck. I was going to cry. I didn't cry.

The last time I'd cried was right after I'd gotten out of hell. I had curled up into a tight ball and let myself wallow in self-pity and sorrow for the loss of Ramiel and my wings.

After that I built a hard wall around myself. I had promised not to let myself become so weak again. That no one would break me. No one.

Now, here I was about to break that promise. I shook my head forcing the tears back. No, I refused.

"Come on, Mary. Just let me explain," Sid's hand came down on my shoulder and I snapped.

Spinning around, I grabbed his hand and twisted. The pain on his face made a small part of me smile. Good.

"I don't want to hear any more of your lies," I spat as he wrestled to get his arm from my grip.

"I've never lied to you," he gasped.

I let go of his hand and crossed my arms over my chest, "You said you were human."

"No," Sid rubbed his hand, "You assumed I was human. There's a difference."

"Semantics. You almost got Trisha killed!" I waved the gun at him.

"Hey, watch it with that thing," he held his hand up in defense, his eyes locked on the weapon pointed in his direction.

"What this?" I stopped waving it and leveled it at him. "What's to stop me from pulling the trigger right now? Huh? You're a demon. You shouldn't be here."

"Neither should you," Sid countered and he was right. Neither of us belonged in this world, but at least I wasn't trying to destroy its inhabitants. Biting my tongue, I didn't lower the gun.

"Do you really think you could kill me, angel?" he said softly.

"Yes," I said, though my voice shook.

"Then," he held his hands out to either side giving me a clear shot of his chest, "Do it. If it will make you feel better, shoot me. Send me to hell. God only knows, I'm going to go there eventually."

I held the gun pointed at him for a few moments and then lowered it. I couldn't do it. He hadn't done anything but omit the truth. He had even helped the cops when his father had wanted him to screw me over.

"See, angel," he stepped closer to me, his eyes locking with mine, "I knew you'd forgive me."

Blinding rage filled me and my hand holding the gun shot out. The butt of the gun connected with Sid's face, throwing him to the ground with a satisfying thud.

God forgives. Nowhere did it say that angels had to.

I spun on my heel, no longer wanting to look at him and came face-to-face with a very awake Asmodeus. My eyes widened as he smiled and then a sharp pain shot through my midsection.

"Game over. I win," he smiled at me, his eyes colored over with power.

Glancing down, the pain became more intense at the sight of the knife he had been playing with earlier, now impaled in my abdomen. With one hand I grabbed the knife and took aim with the other.

Asmodeus' head jolted back, the bullet leaving a hole in his skull. This time his eyes closed and he crumbled to the ground.

Dropping the gun to the floor, I placed my other hand on the hilt of the knife. Just as I was about to yank it out Trisha's alarmed outcry alerted the whole room.

"Mary!"

"Wiles!"

Feet pounded on the concrete and I was surrounded. The edges of my vision darkened and the voices around me muffled until I couldn't make out anything anyone said.

The last thing I saw before I passed out was Sid rushing to my side, his face pinched with worry. I wanted to tell him to fuck off. That it's his dad that'd done it but the words wouldn't form. Instead, my eyes fluttered closed and everything became dark.

20

SOMETIME BETWEEN BEING LOADED into the ambulance and Trisha murmuring to me that everything would be all right, I dreamed.

As usual, it wasn't a pleasant dream. The single light bulb that hung from the ceiling filled my brain. I watched it swing back and forth in the air, the only entertainment I had while I waited for them to come back and torture me again.

I didn't know why they kept coming back. Why didn't they just kill me and get it over with? They never asked me any questions. Never tried to turn me to their side. Not that I knew anything to tell.

I wasn't above begging for death, and I had tried, Lord knew I'd tried. But they never gave it to me. There was only laughter and the pain, the searing torture as they hacked away at the bones in my back, the screams that ripped from my throat as they sliced my wings from my back, and the jeering agony in my side.

Wait. They hadn't done anything to my side. The darkened room faded and a beeping sound filled my ears.

"I think she's waking up," Trisha's voice said next to me, "Come on, Mare, don't die on me. Who's going to hire me if you're gone? You know what a pain in the ass I am."

"You got that right," I grumbled, my eyes flickering open and then quickly closing at the bright light of the room. Since I was no longer in the ambulance and the softness beneath me was unlike that of the gurney they had driven me away in, I could only assume I had made it to the hospital. Opening my eyes again, this time slowly, the first person I saw was Trisha leaning over me.

Her usual dark makeup was smeared. She had trails of mascara and eyeliner down the sides of her face as if she had been crying. It made my heart clench. She'd been that worried about me?

"Hey," Trisha murmured, rubbing the hand she had clasped in hers, "How are you feeling?"

"Like I got stabbed," I answered gruffly.

"Well, you are lucky to be alive," an unfamiliar voice said from the other side of me.

I slowly turned my head from Trisha to the voice. Standing on the other side of the bed was a short stout man with a shaved head. His eyes watched me intently over the glasses that sat on his nose, as if I were some great mystery he needed to figure out. Little did he know I probably was.

"Who are you?" I croaked.

"I'm Doctor Ryan," he answered, "I've been overseeing your care since you arrived early last evening. And I have to say, you are remarkable."

"I've been out that long?" I cleared my throat and searched around for something to drink.

"Here," Trisha pushed a button on the bed that made me move up into a semi-sitting position. I was happy not to be lying down anymore but it made my side ache. I tried to take the water Trisha

257

offered me but my hand came up short and stung.

I frowned at my hand. They had placed something on my finger and stuck a needle in the top of my hand. Before I could ask, Trisha said, "The nurse put those on. This one," she pointed at the device on my finger, "monitors your pulse and oxygen levels. While this one," she pointed at the needle in my hand, "makes sure you get enough fluids."

"Don't worry, you'll be able to take them out once we are sure you are out of the woods and can be discharged. It's not every day someone survives a knife wound to the liver without needing surgery." the doctor said.

I kept my face straight at the accusation in his voice, "I'm a fast healer I guess."

"Apparently, so," he pursed his lips, not quite liking my answer, "Well, we did stitch you up and while you could go home now, we would like to keep you a bit longer to run some tests," he folded his hands over each other in front of him. "Like I said before, Miss Wiles, you are a modern miracle."

"That's all well and good, but I think I'll just go home now."

"Are you sure?" he lifted a brow, "I really do insist you stay longer. Just in case there are any complications we missed."

"Yeah, I'm sure," I didn't need some doctor checking into my biology. There was no telling what he would find. The fact that he had some of my blood from the injury was already worrying. The world was not ready to know that angels, let alone demons, really existed. And I wasn't going to be the one responsible for it getting leaked.

"I'll get your stuff ready. Can we get the discharge papers?" Trisha looked to Doctor Ryan, her expression telling him he'd better not argue with her.

"I'll have a nurse bring them in," he reluctantly said, "but, you need to take it easy. No strenuous activity. No stress. And you need to keep those stitches clean," he pointed at my side where it began to ache like it knew it was being talked about, "You'll need to come back in a few weeks to get the stitches removed."

"Got it," I nodded, shifting on the bed so that I was on the side next to Trisha, "Can

259

I get this stuff taken off now?" I held my hand covered in wires up.

"Yes, I'll have the nurse remove that as well. I want it on the record that you are leaving against doctor's advisement," he tried once more to convince me to stay.

"Understood," I leveled him with a look, showing I wasn't going to back down from this.

"Fine," his jaw clenched until I thought it might pop from its socket and then he settled his gaze on Trisha, "Make sure she doesn't pull those stitches. I don't want to have to sew her back up."

"You got it," Trisha mock saluted him, which only seemed to infuriate him more as he marched out of the room, his white lab coat whipping around behind him.

"Are you okay? Really?" Trisha asked once he was out of earshot.

I gave her a weak smile. "I'm fine. I'm an angel, remember?"

"A former angel," she reminded me, "which you'll have to explain to me at some point how you were keeping this big secret from me and I didn't even suspect anything."

"No one knew."

"Sidney did," Trisha accused.

I didn't respond as she helped me pull on my pants. Each movement was like I was being stabbed all over again. I was an angel, yeah. I healed fast, but that didn't mean it didn't still hurt like a bitch.

"He came by, you know. To check on you."

I couldn't answer because the nurse walked in at that moment. I gave Trisha a warning look as the elderly lady came over to our side of the bed.

"Well, you are an independent thing, aren't you?" she tut-tutted at me and gestured for me to sit back down on the bed, "Let's get you fixed up, shall we?"

The nurse set about taking the wires off and the needle out of my hand, which didn't hurt as much as sting when she removed it. She bandaged the hand up and then checked my vitals before handing me a stack of papers.

"You need to fill these out so you can be discharged. We'll need your insurance, health history, and an emergency contact," she pointed to each line of the page as she said them.

"All right," I stared down at the papers, confusion riddling my face.

The nurse took pity on me and patted me on the shoulder, "I'll just come back for those in a little bit," as soon as she was gone, Trisha was back at it.

"So, about Sid."

"What about him?" I winced as I raised my arms to pull my shirt over my head. This was going to suck big time.

"Are you going to go talk to him?" she knelt on the ground to help me put my boots on, "he was pretty worried about you."

"He shouldn't be. I'm fine."

"All right, if you say so," Trisha sat in the chair by the bed and started working on the forms that the nurse had brought in. I wouldn't have a clue what to put down on there, that's why I loved having Trisha around so much. Except when she brought up undesirable topics.

I didn't want to talk about Sid or his betrayal. The list of people I trusted in this city was short. Trisha, Adara, sometimes Thompson, and until last night, Sid. Now I didn't know what to think.

This whole time he had been lying to my face. I mean, I hadn't outright asked him if he was a demon, or even a half demon, but he knew what I was, so it was only a courtesy for him to give me a head's up.

If I'd known, I wouldn't have . . . I wouldn't have what? Flirted with him? Not pretended I only came to his bar for work when I really just wanted to see him?

No.

If I'd known he was a demon, even only half demon, I wouldn't have even talked to him if I could have helped it. I couldn't exorcise him since he wasn't possessed, but that didn't mean I couldn't stop him from hurting people.

But *was* he hurting people?

I'd never seen him doing anything remotely demon-like. Sure, sometimes he was moody, which made me now realize that it was probably his demon side trying to come to the surface. Thinking of it reminded me of when he had taken that couple to the back room.

If his father was the demon of lust, then what did that make him? The bar always had a sensual type feeling to it, and his looks, as Trisha would say, screamed sex,

263

I didn't understand how I hadn't seen it before. I felt like such an idiot.

"I'm putting the LAPD down for insurance," Trisha's voice interrupted my thoughts, "They got you stabbed, the least they can do is foot the bill."

"That's fine," I said, not really understanding the whole insurance bit. Having to pay for health care was unreasonable to me. In heaven, I was a soldier and a healer. I never expected anyone to pay me to save their life. Not many angels' lives were in jeopardy, but the occasional demon attack did happen while visiting earth.

"Who should I put down for your emergency contact?"

"Si—" I caught myself before I said his name and then said, "Just put your name down."

"Are you sure?" her brows rose, "I'm not even old enough to drink, you really want to put your life in my hands?"

I shrugged, "I have no one else, and you are hardly incompetent. If I can't trust you, who can I trust?"

The nurse from before came in leaving my question unanswered. "You must have an admirer. These were left at the front desk," she handed me a bouquet of orange water lilies. Instantly my stomach twisted at the sight of them. Only one person knew what flower I liked.

Not even thanking her, I searched the bundle for a card. Anything to confirm my thoughts.

"Here," Trisha offered me a small white rectangle, "This fell on the floor."

I reached out and then I hesitated. Swallowing thickly, I took the card from her and turned it over.

Get well soon. ~R

My heart pounded in my chest and I felt as if I might faint. It couldn't be. It's a trick. A lie. But why would anyone pretend to be him? Messing with me like this seemed childish even for demons.

I stared down at the card again.

R? Could it really be him? I had thought Asmodeus had been lying. That he was just trying to trick me so that he could have Trisha, but what if he was telling the truth? Otherwise, how would he even know where to find me or that I was even on earth?

"Who's it from?" Trisha asked, her eyes on my shocked face.

I met her gaze and barely breathed out, "Ramiel."

"What?" she jumped up grabbing the card from my lax fingers. She mouthed the words on the card and turned it over, seemingly to see if there was anything more to it, but when there wasn't she turned to me, "What does this mean?"

"It means," I cleared my throat, "That Asmodeus was telling the truth. Ramiel is alive and he's here."

Trisha placed a hand on her hip, "So what now?"

What indeed? He hadn't left any kind of contact information so it was obvious he didn't want me to find him, or contact him. But that was just tough shit.

I didn't get trapped on earth to live a normal, ordinary existence. I did it for him and if he's been alive and well this whole time, he had some explaining to do.

Standing from the bed, I moved past Trisha to grab my leather jacket. I hissed as I dragged it on but pushed back the pain. Taking the papers from Trisha's hands, I started out of the room.

266

"Miss Wiles," Doctor Ryan said when he saw me, "Have you reconsidered?"

"Nope," I shoved the papers into his hands and kept walking. I didn't stop even when he called out after me. I had more important things to do than play lab-rat for an egotistical doctor.

"Trisha," I called over my shoulder, having no doubt that she was following behind me, "I need you to see if you can trace who purchased those flowers. See if you can get an address. A phone number. Anything."

Trisha half ran to catch up with my long legs. "What are we hunting this time boss?"

I smirked as I made my way out of the hospital, "An archangel."

Ramiel might not want to be found but finding people was what I specialized in. Demons, cheating spouses—and now even archangels—had better watch out, Mary Wiles was out for blood.

Bound By Hell

In the City of Lost Angels, keep your friends close and your demons closer...

For a millennia Mary Wiles played the good guy. Stay on the path and all would be well. But now that she has long strayed from that path there is nothing stopping her from hunting down those who hurt her.

To save a fellow angel, Mary will have to break all the rules. Unfortunately, that means asking for help from a half-demon she had once called friend.

She'll have to pay a heavy price to find what was lost: help a demon cross over to the human plane. But the closer she gets to completing her task the deeper she gets entangled by their lies. Soon, Mary realizes that not even angels can stave off the fires of hell forever.

ABOUT THE AUTHOR

Erin Bedford is a *USA Today* bestselling fantasy and paranormal romance author, a computer programmer by day, and a hobby hoarder.
Creating fantastical worlds have always been a secret passion of hers and she couldn't imagine writing any story without some kind of lovey-dovey or smexy goodness in it.

Read More from Erin Bedford
www.erinbedford.com

www.ingramcontent.com/pod-product-compliance
Lightning Source LLC
Chambersburg PA
CBHW071749190726
48292CB00003B/915